subway
girl

subway
girl

P. J. CONVERSE

HARPER TEEN
An Imprint of HarperCollinsPublishers

HarperTeen is an imprint of HarperCollins Publishers.

Subway Girl
Copyright © 2011 by Peter Jacob Converse

Library of Congress Cataloging-in-Publication Data
Converse, Peter Jacob.
     p. cm.
   Summary: In Hong Kong, Chan Tze Man, called Simon Chan, leaves high school because he cannot master English, but when he befriends Amy, a Chinese American who knows little Chinese, their unlikely bond gives hope to both.
   ISBN 978-0-06-157514-3
   [1. Friendship—Fiction. 2. Language and languages—Fiction. 3. Dating (Social customs)—Fiction. 4. High schools—Fiction. 5. Schools—Fiction. 6. Family life—China—Fiction. 7. Hong Kong (China)—Fiction. 8. China—Fiction.] I. Title.
PZ7.C7682Sub 2011   2010007026
[Fic]—dc22   CIP
                                                                                          AC

Typography by Sasha Illingworth
11 12 13 14 15   LP/RRDB   10 9 8 7 6 5 4 3 2 1
❖
First Edition

To my mother

subway
girl

1

The bell jingled. The shop door creaked open, and a whiff of bus engines came through to Chan Tze Man, still in bed, waiting till the last moment to get up for school. "Ahh," he said, and he breathed in deep, though not as deep as when he was younger and believed the smell was baked bread. He slid off his top bunk with a light heart, then remembered what the school day had in store for him.

"Oh, my mother," he groaned, and looked for his uniform. Chan Tze Man, or Simon Chan to his English teachers and his friend Katie, lived in the back of his parents' odds-and-ends shop near the Tai Wo Hau subway station. Tai Wo Hau was a shabby residential area on the outskirts of Hong Kong. It had been in the news once for having the first underground train station, but that was a long time ago. Now only locals stopped there.

In his tiny room, Simon put on two worn-out sweaters and an elastic school tie. Then he crouched down to check himself in his Spider-Man mirror, impressed by how the tape had held it there for so long. Beside it was an old poster of Heathrow, the world's greatest airport. He'd read that people who wanted to travel around the world needed to pass through its great hub. If only he could still make it there, he thought. But how?

He picked up his bag and stepped through hanging beads into the dim, dusty light of aisle number one. Familiar bowls, spoons, brooms, mugs, hangers, hooks, mirrors, pencil sharpeners, and instant noodles seemed to whisper their disappointment in him as he walked by. *Chaaan, what happened to yooooou? We believed in yooooou.*

When he reached the front of the store, Simon noticed his elderly parents in aisle number two, Mr. Chan was with the butterfly nets, Mrs. Chan with the cans of insecticide.

"Will you graduate?" asked his mother.

"Huh?" replied Simon, startled, before remembering it was what she asked on other mornings too.

"Life begins when school finishes!" added his father, like a madman waking from a coma, and he then began to laugh.

"What?" said Simon. "Dad?"

But his parents' thoughts had returned to their shop, and all recognition of an outside world was gone.

He took a deep breath and answered his mother anyway. "I think I'm going to fail out of school and I don't know what I'm going to do."

"The top shelf is too high for your father," said Mrs. Chan.

"But—"

"Come back early for the counting."

"Where is my calculator?" shouted Mr. Chan.

"You don't need a calculator!" shouted Mrs. Chan. "Leave them! Chan Tze Man will count!"

"Wha-aht?!" spat his father.

"Stop arguing!" screamed his mother.

"Bye," said Simon as the bell jangled behind him.

The human current began two steps in front of their shop. Cleaners, secretaries, clerks, teachers, school kids and men with crumpled racing guides were all headed to the trains. The students in uniforms were the best dressed, many decorated with prize badges and pins. Simon let two gray-suit-wearing kindergarten students pass by, then slung back his schoolbag and entered the crowd, even less aware of the crush than usual.

Today was the day his class got back its mock English exam, the exam that showed what a person could hope for on the big public exam soon to follow. Few students in Simon's year expected to do well enough to be promoted to Form 6[1], but most expected to at least pass and finish school with Hong Kong's basic qualification, the Leaving Certificate. Simon was almost positive he hadn't passed the mock, and he was thinking about all the bad things that meant. In Hong Kong, you could be the next Confucius and you still wouldn't get your Leaving Certificate if you failed English. Maybe the next Confucius was sweeping the streets somewhere, saying beautiful and wise things in Chinese only.

It wasn't that he hadn't tried. It was just that the English syllabus was for students who had English-speaking parents, English-speaking Filipina nannies, or private tutors, while Simon's parents spoke two words of English—"okay, okay"—and saw no need to pay someone to teach their son any more than that. Simon had gotten used to failing English tests, but failing out of school was going to be a new experience.

He rode two escalators down to his platform, walked over to where the third carriage stopped, and waited at the back of the line. The second door of the third carriage lined up with the middle escalator at Mongkok station where he got off. That way, as soon as the train stopped he'd have to take only a few quick strides and he'd be about the third person to the escalator. Otherwise he'd get lost in a mass of

---

[1] Form 6 equals Grade 12.

at least a hundred people reaching the escalator at the same time.

Once on the train, getting a seat wasn't an issue. People from his station rarely got to sit. The flat steel benches were all taken before Tai Wo Hau. First to go were the two-seaters, then the end seats on the six-seaters, and finally the middle seats on the six-seaters. Usually a couple of guys would try to sit with their knees splayed out and make a six-seater into a five or even a four. But by the time the train got to Simon's station, normally an old lady would have made the guys move their legs. Then there would be six across from that point until the end of the line.

For once, Simon looked carefully at the adult passengers on his train. Which one? he thought to himself. Which one will be me? Probably no one, he decided. Maybe the ones who failed school didn't even take the train. Where would they have to go?

Maybe they were rounded up from their families and let loose in desert areas. Or maybe they were just taken away and shot after answering one final grammar question incorrectly.

"You, what is the past tense of 'to lay'?"

"Lied? Lain? Can joo repeat?"

"Fire!"

Simon chuckled quietly. Laugh while you can, he thought as the train jerked to a stop. Then he moved out of the way of the opening door and saw Subway Girl walk in.

She moved to the dark section in between the carriages, earphones in. As usual, Simon forgot everything he was thinking, and tried to stop looking at her before she turned around.

He'd still never seen her come on with anyone, or even talk to anyone from her school. Most of the girls in her uniform hung out in the first and second carriages.

A lot of people talked about her, though. She was kind of famous with the guys who took the train. Spotting her at the station had become a game. Simon thought she had to notice, but she never showed it.

He liked that about her. He liked the way she didn't seem bothered by what other people were doing, and how she seemed happy to be by herself. And he liked how she didn't dress up her uniform or put cutesy cartoon stickers on her bag. She wore socks instead of stockings. Her shoes were scuffed. She had purple streaks in her black hair. To Simon, she was the coolest and most beautiful girl he had ever seen. And he knew if he was ever going to ask a girl out, she was the one he had to ask.

But she never looked like she wanted to talk to anyone. She always wore earphones and she kept her eyes closed a lot. And after six months of thinking about what he was going to say, he'd come up with nothing.

Okay, thought Simon, if I pass the English mock, I'll say hello and ask her out . . . for boba in Mongkok . . . or something. I'll still be numb with shock, so it won't matter if she tells me to go away. If I don't pass, there won't be a reason to say anything anyway because my life would be over. Okay then! Done. Wednesday, March 14 could end up being the worst or possibly the best day ever.

2

Simon Chan sat three floors above the canteen in the back of room 306, looking out the window and nervously tapping his fingers.

His English teacher, Mr. Lam, was walking along the third-floor balcony with the school's newest teacher, and first-ever American, Mr. Jack Slaughter. Mr. Lam's squat frame was partially hidden behind a bundle of exam papers.

"Mr. Slaughter! Mr. Slaughter! How are you today? Will you teach our class?" a band of girl students called out.

"You are like a rock star," said Mr. Lam. "Everyone wants to speak to you."

"No-o," replied the American modestly.

"English class Number One," said the veteran teacher, nodding toward a room full of quietly working students. "Most of their parents speak English quite well. English class Number Two is also quite reasonable."

"I see," said the American, glimpsing at the slightly noisier rows of raised hands. The two did not pause at Number Three, where a microphoned teacher had temporarily broken into angry Chinese.

Mr. Lam's class, Number Four, was much farther down, its door just before the far stairwell.

"I feel like we're walking deep into the jungle," said the American.

"Ha-ha. Yes," said veteran Lam.

Not many of the students called the American's name as he entered the class. Saying his name would have been speaking English, and few in Number Four ever did so voluntarily.

"So which class am I getting?" Mr. Slaughter asked.

"Number Five," said Mr. Lam.

"Jesus," said the American, causing a few students to look up.

The older teacher smiled. "Don't worry. They are not so demanding and we don't expect a miracle. You'll only be teaching them for a short time before they must leave to prepare for their Certificate examination."

"Well, that sounds all right, then."

"Students," announced Mr. Lam.

Finally, thought Simon.

"Before I give back your exams, I must hear one discussion. Leon! Andy! Kenny! Simon."

"Oh man." Simon winced. English discussions were the worst. Every one was the same: painful and pointless.

The boys walked to the front and took their places around the discussion table.

Simon began, "Today we are discussing . . ." Then he looked at the discussion topic for the first time and decided not to paraphrase. "The principal of your school is going to invite a guest speaker to talk about his or her career and has suggested either an airline pilot, a sportsman/sportswoman, or a newspaper reporter."

"Good point," said Andy.

"I'm agree with that," said Leon.

"Let's move on," said Kenny.

"Look at the list of things to talk about!" said Mr. Lam.

"'Interesting things about the careers,'" read Simon.

"I think playing sport is very interesting," said Leon.

"I'm agree with you," said Andy.

"Let's move on," said Kenny.

"Yes, I'm agree with you," said Leon. "What is your opinion, Simon?"

Simon shrugged. "Opinion about what?"

"Thank you, Simon," said Kenny.

"I'm agree with you," said Leon.

"Good point," said Andy.

The class began to snicker.

"I want to hear a suggestion!" Mr. Lam demanded.

Leon shifted in his seat, then looked away from the table. Kenny whispered to Simon in Chinese. "Say a suggestion so we can go."

"I don't have a suggestion," Simon whispered back. But a moment later, Simon said in English, "I want to invite the airline pilot because his life is interesting."

"Whoa," went the class, impressed. Then the American spoke and everyone went quiet again.

"Why? Why do you think a pilot's life would be interesting?"

"He will go to many places," Simon mumbled.

"Would you like to travel?" continued the American.

Simon shrugged. He didn't like to talk about personal things in class, especially not in English class.

"Yes," he said, blushing.

"Good," said Mr. Lam, now ready to hand out the exam. "Your English is improving. Maybe your result will also improve this time."

Simon began to feel queasy with hope. The new teacher stretched.

"Chan Ka Hung," said Mr. Lam and handed back the first paper.

"Ivy Chow."

"Forty-eight percent!" said Ivy.

"Show me," said Eric, the nosy guy.

"Emily Wah."

"Fifty-one! Oh my god!"

"Genius," said Eric. "Let me see."

"Karen Lao."

Simon was trying to recall his feeling at "pens down." Had he been confident? Relaxed?

"Sylvia Mak."

Bored, he remembered, because he'd finished early and decided it was pointless to check his answers. Nothing ever looked right anyway.

"Simon Chan. Better."

Holy mother, thought Simon. I've done it. "Thank you," he said as he took his paper.

"Wow," said Eric as he read the result over Simon's shoulder. "That sucks."

A thirty-nine. Simon stared at the number for a moment and then went through the motions of putting his exam in his bag, putting his bag over his shoulder, and moving toward the door. "Better?" Better than what?

"Students who got below forty percent," the teacher announced, "for the rest of the year you will join Mr.

Slaughter in Number Five."

A couple of girls giggled. Simon felt a ringing in his ears.

"That's it," he said. "I'm never speaking English again. Somebody shoot me if I speak it again."

3

"*Simon!*" came the familiar voice as he stepped into the lane behind the school. It was followed by a chubby-handed slap on the back.

"What do *you* want?" he said without turning around.

"Where are you headed?" said his oldest friend, ignoring his tone.

"Nowhere."

"Let's go somewhere," said Katie.

"Where to?"

"I want to go to Portugal. I want to meet Cristiano Ronaldo."

"Who? What's so great about him?"

"I love him."

"Okay, then, let's go."

They'd been friends since the first Morning Prayer in Form 1. Simon had said they were like goats and Katie had started to baa. She became half of his plans to travel the world, but things had changed.

"Wait a minute," she said as a few of her classmates passed by. Mr. Popularity, Steven Lai, was in the lead.

"Steven!" Katie called out. "What did you get for English?"

"Seventy percent," he replied without stopping.

"I hate you!"

"'I hate you,'" Steven's friends mimicked, then called out that she should have some more fish balls.

Katie acted like she hadn't heard but Simon could tell she had. He wanted to yell something back, but knew Katie wouldn't like it.

"Steven's so smart," she said a moment later.

"Not as smart as you."

"Hey, do you really think I can pass?"

"Yes."

"But my grammar is so terrible."

"You passed the mock, right?"

"Yeah, barely."

"I told you. You're the best, Katie."

"We're the best, remember?"

Simon rolled his eyes.

It was true that he'd been a keen English student once. But that was back when he was twelve, back when he thought anything was possible.

Neither of them had been naturals at English, but Simon figured that if they tried harder than everybody else, they could make it to one of the top English classes, and hang on until they graduated. After that, the sky would be the limit—even university. So they took notes, did all their homework, and filled shoeboxes with vocabulary cards. But in Form 4, when the Certificate syllabus began, Simon couldn't keep up.

Over the summer, many of his classmates had either spoken English overseas or gone to study schools, and almost all of them had hired a tutor, even Katie. Simon asked his parents if he could have one too, but they didn't see the point.

"School is for rich people and doctors!" his father had declared.

Katie offered to take her private lessons at a library so Simon could join her without her parents finding out. Simon thought he would get her in trouble, so he told her he was fine.

But he wasn't fine. No matter how hard he studied, he couldn't keep all the new words and grammar in his head. It seemed like whatever English you studied would disappear as soon as you walked back out into the Chinese world. His English never sounded right, and the more he studied, the more confused he became.

He began to worry about things he never previously worried about. Like if you made adverbs by adding "ly" to adjectives, why couldn't you say "I worked hardly" instead of "I worked hard"? Why did so many words sound different from the way they were spelled? Simon couldn't even figure out the difference between "I am *bored*" and "I am *boring*."

Katie cried when he was moved down to a lower class after the first midterm.

"It's not like I'm moving schools," he told her, but it almost was. The top English students had longer classes. They studied together, hung out together, sung in the English choir together, and planned for Form 6 together.

Simon just hoped that Katie wouldn't bring up his English exam. He wasn't in the mood to talk about it.

"So?"

"So what?"

"What did you get on your English exam?"

"Forget it."

"How close?"

"Not close."

"Simon! You said you would try!"

"Look, I can't. I can't do English."

"But—"

"Katie!"

She looked away.

He looked down.

"We can still go overseas," he said in a gentler voice. "Just maybe stow away."

"Shut up," she told him, but she smiled this time despite herself.

They walked the last few steps to the footbridge in silence. It was where Katie crossed over to the local housing estates.

"You never know," said Katie as she started up the steps.

"Know what?" asked Simon.

Katie shook her head.

"Don't give up," she called out in English.

Simon acted like the words caused him pain as he walked on down the road.

4

Mongkok was as bustling as ever. It was impossible to even walk in a straight line, but he liked it that way. It was cool seeing people from different schools going in and out of cafés, dawdling in front of shops, paying attention to bargains and girlfriends, and dodging minibuses.

He took the middle stairs down to Mongkok station, away from the beggars and the family of cheap-toy salesmen on the edges, and tried not to look for Subway Girl. He focused on shop signs, light fixtures, a magazine cover.

It was possible that he'd never see her again. There were only four more weeks of school. She could take an earlier train every time or a later one. The trains were only five minutes apart. It's for the best, he thought. It was time to stop daydreaming about Heathrow Airport—about being the first in his family to get to Form 6, and about her. Then he spotted the earphoned one walking toward his turnstile and forgot everything.

By the time he reached the line, she was already through and at the top of the escalator. He watched her until she disappeared, then imagined running after her. At the bottom of the escalator, he caught up.

"I was wondering when you were going to say hello," she said. "What took you so long?"

"I don't know, I . . ."

"It's been driving me crazy. I'm so sick of this game we've been playing."

"I know, I know."

"Chan."

"You know my name."

"Chan!"

"Yes, I'm Chan."

"Chan, wake up."

"Huh?"

"You're blocking the line."

It was Eric from English class Number Four beside the heavyset Raymond Wah of Number Three.

"You got below forty, didn't you?" said Eric, as Simon beeped through. "I was just telling—"

"I see her! Subway Girl," called Raymond, from the escalator.

"Let's go!" said Eric.

But a train arrived and the platform congealed into solid lines. The three of them just managed to squeeze on as the warning bell rang.

"Steven told me he saw her in Tsim Sha Tsui on Saturday night," Raymond said proudly.

"Was she with a boyfriend?" asked Eric.

"He didn't say. Why don't you ask her? Maybe she's going to choose you."

"Why don't you?"

"She doesn't talk to anyone. That's why."

"She's too stuck-up," said Eric.

"She's a ho if you ask me," said Raymond. "I've seen girls like her. They like older guys."

Eric snickered. "I don't think she's so good-looking anyway. She has some pimples and her hair's weird."

Simon shook his head.

The stations went by as quickly as usual. At Cheung Sha Wan, Eric and Raymond got off and Simon sat down in one of their empty seats. Soon he'd be home counting stock. He'd start in the second aisle. Pencil or pen? he wondered. Pencils got blunt but pens were messy and he always had to adjust figures at some point. Pencil, then. He'd get one of the reloadable ones if he had enough change. He shifted in his seat to search his back pocket and saw a glimpse of purple-streaked hair.

"Oh, man," he mumbled, and felt the same feeling in his stomach that he always felt before he came up with a reason not to go over. This is stupid, thought Simon. I'm going to fail out of school. I won't even be on the subway for long. Just sit back and forget her.

But he couldn't. Deep down, he knew that he'd never forgive himself if he didn't try, and the longer he sat there the worse he felt.

I'll do it. I'll get rid of all hope on the same Wednesday. He grabbed his bag and stood up.

Whoa, he thought. Cool. Then the panic set in.

There were three stops to go before she got off. Only a few minutes left to figure out what to say.

Hey, I'm Chan Tze Man. Hi, I'm Chan Tze Man.

Hi. Hey there.

I've been meaning to say hello to you but . . . I've been meaning to say hello to you but . . . I've just . . .

Do you mind if I ask you a few questions?

Hi. Hey there. Yo.

He looked out into the darkness as the train entered the last tunnel before Lai King. It was like the end of an English exam and "pens down" was coming up. He knew he'd have to settle on something, but what? Everything sounded so obvious, so dumb. He had to think extra hard and quickly.

Hi, I'm Chan Tze Man and I'm failing out of school. To-morrow I will go to the bottom class. I hope the new textbook can improve my English. It is called English for Farm Animal.

English, he thought. At least he didn't have to come up with something in that crazy language. English. . . . ENGLISH! THAT'S IT!

All he had to do was look up from a textbook, shake his head, and say, "English." Every Hong Kong student could relate to that. There was so much to dislike! Yeah!

But when did he carry around an English textbook?

The train jerked to a halt and Simon moved over to the side where she stood.

Then the passengers poured in and started to push Simon closer and closer.

Oh, not good, thought Simon when the train took off again. Now they were too close. His face was ten centimeters from Subway Girl's head. Suddenly a hand reached behind her to free some strands of purple-streaked hair. It looked like her earphones had gotten tangled.

"Shit," she said.

It was the first word he'd ever heard her say. In English.

5

"*Too many people,*" Simon said quietly.

"So many people," he said, a little louder.

Again she didn't reply, but a guy to his left grunted in agreement.

He decided to fish some papers out of his bag. One of them had to be an English exercise.

At first nothing came, so he pulled at the whole tangled mess and out popped his discount MP3 player, which then crashed to the floor.

He'd forgotten the thing was in his bag. It worked only now and then. He dropped his bag on his shoes and tried to bend down without headbutting anyone, and then a small miracle happened. Subway Girl nudged his MP3 player toward him with her foot.

When he stood back up, she was looking at its lit-up screen.

"Thank you," he said.

She smiled and took a closer look at what was playing.

He looked at the exercises in his other hand and shook his head.

"English," he said, in Chinese.

"That's exactly what I'm listening to," she said in English.

"What?" he asked, in Chinese.

"I love that song," she continued in English.

He looked at the song. It was by a foreign band, the Black Peas or something. Someone must've thought it was cool and uploaded it for him at school. He didn't have a computer at home.

Simon laughed. "Oh, you think because of this song that I speak English?"

"I'm sorry. Could you say that in English?" she said.

Then Simon's temples began to throb. "You don't . . . You cannot speak Chinese?" he said finally, in English.

"No. I'm sorry," she said. "I thought because of the song maybe you spoke English too. Doesn't matter. I'm sorry." And she began to turn away.

"Yes . . . I like English," he said, and began to choke a little.

"You do?" she said, not completely convinced. "I just don't like to put people through it."

"You are not Chinese?" Simon said.

"Well, sort of. Chinese American."

"Oh," he said. She wasn't stuck-up at all. She was an English speaker, which was worse. "Your parents. They are Chinese?"

"Yeah. They're from here."

"They can speak Chinese."

"Uh-huh."

"But they did not teach you?"

"Nope, not really."

"Now you are here."

"Yep." She smiled politely and started to fiddle with her iPod. It looked like they'd reached the end of their exchange. "Well, I hope yours isn't broken," she said.

Simon racked his brain for another English question. "You are here for long time?"

"Um . . . You mean how long have I been here?"

"Yes."

"About six months."

"I see."

She touched her iPod again.

"What is . . . ," he began as she brought up one earphone. "Sorry," he said. "Never mind."

"It's okay. What is what?" she said.

"What is your opinion of Hong Kong?"

As soon as he'd said it, he thought of the oral examination and Chris Wong, the fictitious interviewer. You are pesky Chris Wong, he told himself.

"I like it," she replied. "Sort of. I'm still getting used to it. It's very interesting."

"Yes, Hong Kong is very interesting," said Simon.

"Yeah, so interesting," she repeated and slightly rolled her eyes. Simon's heart sank. But then she gave a playful laugh. "What about you? What is 'your opinion'?"

"I think okay," said Simon, "but I don't know other places."

"Yeah," she said, "I know what you mean."

He couldn't believe he was actually speaking English. It was exhilarating, and a little dangerous, like the first time he'd gotten up on a two-wheeler, although back then his problem was speeding out of control, whereas now the challenge was to go fast enough so that his conversation wouldn't wobble and crash.

"What country are you come from before here?" he continued.

"The U.S."

"U.S.," he said. "Very big."

"Mm-hmm. But not so crowded."

"Yes, Hong Kong has many people. Mongkok. So terrible."

"I love Mongkok," she said.

"Really?"

"Yeah, it's great."

He loved it too, but it seemed dumb to say so now. "What do you do?" was his next question.

"What do I do?" she giggled. "I live at home with my mother and little brother and I go to school. What about you?"

"I go to school." He laughed.

"Is your school in Mongkok?"

"No. Is your school?"

"Close. I think we're in Yau Ma Tei. Off some main road. I don't know. Our Holy Mother. Something like that."

"I saw other girls who wear your uniform."

"Yeah, it's only girls," she said. "What about you? Just boys?"

"Boys and girls. Male and female . . . and teachers."

She laughed.

Chan Tze Man makes joke in English and girl laughs!

"What form are you in?" she asked. "Form 6?"

"No."

"I am. Back in the U.S., I'd be just about finished. We only go up to twelfth grade . . . I mean Form 6. Here you have to do a year after that, too. It sucks."

Simon nodded. "You like the subway?" he asked, changing the subject.

"Sorry?" she said. "It's all right. So, what about you? When will you finish?"

"This year."

"So you're in Form 7?"

"No. Form 5."

"Oh. Don't you want to go on?"

"Uh . . . I . . . uh . . ."

"It's okay," she said. "I'm just nosy. The subway's fine as long as you have something to listen to. Something loud."

"It's very . . . noise . . ." He broke off as they entered the station tunnel.

"So, what else do you listen to?" she asked as she zipped up her bag.

The only English songs that came to his mind were "I Left My Heart in San Francisco" and the song from the movie *Titanic*. He pointed to his MP3 player, which unfortunately had turned off again. "I like that one."

"Yeah, Black Eyed Peas are great," she said and nodded politely.

"I don't know songs," he blurted out as the train stopped, not wanting the last thing he told her to be a lie. "I don't listen to English songs much. My English is . . ." He shook his head.

"No, it's good," she told him. "It's . . . well, my Chinese is . . . Lei Ho Ma?"

"I'm very good. And you?" he replied in Chinese.

"Sorry?" she said. "I should learn more! Bye." And she disappeared into the crowds.

Five minutes later, Simon was still staring out the train window, happy and dumb as a rock.

6

The next morning Simon filed into school just like every other day, but on the inside he was different. All because of Subway Girl. Even though he hadn't gotten her name and she didn't speak Chinese, they'd talked and she sort of knew him now. Suddenly he wasn't just one of the hundreds who took the same train. It made him feel more optimistic about life in general even with all six classes to go.

Thursday was double Chinese, recess, biology, physical education, lunch, and double English.

Chinese was okay because Mr. Ho demanded full attention and it was hard to think about other things in his class. In biology, however, the teacher let students drift off, then spoke loudly every ten minutes or so. It was like a night of bad sleep. Long before the bell, Simon started to think about his poor English conversation skills more than his exam skills—and whether he'd ever see Subway Girl again.

Inside the phys ed changing rooms, lockers slammed open, the reek of piss overpowered the smell of sweat, and the subject changed to girls and the graduation party.

"Hey, Eric, who are you taking?" asked Steven Lai, who already knew the answer was nobody.

"I think it's better to go in a group," said Eric.

"Of course you do." Steven laughed.

"Who are you going with, Steven?" asked one of his cronies.

"I'm still thinking. Is Katie free? I like girls who are fat and ugly!"

Everybody laughed except Simon.

"Oh, wait," said Steven. "I forgot that her boyfriend is here. I hope you have fun together. Don't forget your leash, Chan."

More laughter.

"So original," said Simon.

"Steven should ask Long-Legs Lao," said Raymond.

Steven jutted his chin in the direction of one of their year's basketball stars. "She's going with Marc, dickhead."

"What about Queen Rachel, then?"

Catcalls and kissing sounds filled the room.

"Maybe," Steven said. "I haven't decided."

"What about Subway Girl?" asked Eric.

Oohs and ahhs.

"Now you're talking."

"You mean fantasy girl," said one of the guys who never took the train.

Simon's ears pricked up.

"She's not a fantasy," replied Eric. "I saw her yesterday."

"Forget it!" Marc shouted over the cheers.

"Why?"

"I've seen her at clubs. I've seen who she goes out with."

"Who?"

"Not high school kids."

"I don't care," said Steven. "I know what girls want."

The guys hooted.

"Go for it!"

"Ask her!"

"Just don't say you're in Form 5."

"Obviously," Steven said as he headed out.

Simon checked his locker for nothing in particular, then shut it for good. It was stupid to be upset about Subway Girl, but he couldn't help it. At least she wouldn't be interested in Steven, either. Of course she wouldn't care about someone in high school, let alone in Form 5. Her boyfriend was probably a young pilot or a scientist or at least a millionaire. He shook his head. School always made him feel worse about life. Then the lunch bell rang.

"Do you think you have to dance at the graduation party?" Simon asked a couple of Form 2s.

The four-footers looked at him like he was an idiot. "Yeah."

He wondered if Katie would expect him to if he asked her to go. The other part of the evening would be okay. They always had fun together. Even though only Katie was graduating, it made sense to go to a graduation party to finish things. Some parts of school had been good, just not recently.

7

Amy got out of a minibus in the middle of Mongkok and immediately began to relax. The world seemed large and interesting again. She loved the noise. It seemed to say all the things about life that couldn't be said at school. She drifted with the crowds, avoided delivery trucks and cars, and walked through hanging garments and smoke and the steam from street food.

A girl at school named Elizabeth had asked her for a maxi pad. She'd gotten her period early and wasn't prepared. Amy gave her a tampon and the girl had looked at it like it was a drug and Amy a dealer.

"What?" Amy smiled. "You haven't used one of these before?"

"No!" said Elizabeth.

When she came out of the bathroom, Elizabeth looked like she had a terrible secret inside of her and whispered to Amy that she would never let a guy near her now if that's what it felt like. Amy laughed too but she felt uncomfortable. She wondered how she'd be treated if her classmates knew more about her.

Girls weren't supposed to go on dates at her school, and sex was for married couples and animal species only. Relationships were discussed openly in Christian fellowship meetings, but not the kind of relationships she'd experienced. There were some other girls who had serious boyfriends and went out a lot, but they accepted that what they did was immoral and did it anyway. Amy didn't think she was immoral, but she really needed to walk around Mongkok to remind herself that the world was huge and no one had all the answers.

She loved the wild diversity of Hong Kong. Parts of the city were like pages out of a fashion magazine and other parts were cheap and dirty. And instead of quaint, old Chinatown, there was China up the road. San Francisco seemed sort of small and tame now.

But at the same time, there was this strict girls' school, and her mother was scrutinizing her more than ever. It was like all of a sudden she had to become a modest Asian girl. Was she supposed to suddenly forget that she'd grown up in America? Not all the girls in Hong Kong were all that modest.

Amy put in her earphones and entered the subway. At a little cake shop, she noticed the counter girls were her age and wondered what it would be like to work underground all day instead of just passing through.

Passing through was a trip. Normal speed in the subway station was like the fast-motion shots of city life on TV. She liked to stand still and let her music play the soundtrack to her sensations. It took her mind off the apartment she was speeding to.

She heard children playing, babies wailing, and the murmur of adults as she walked down her hallway. Every family had their TV on. The smell of sesame oil and fried chicken was very strong. She opened a metal screen and unlocked a second door. Her mother and grandmother were talking loudly in the kitchen. Nathan was lying in front of the TV doing his homework. Amy took off her shoes and kicked her brother on the way to her room.

"Hey, bug," she said, as he started barking around her ankles.

"Amy?" her mother called.

She pushed open her door. A man was sitting on her bed.

"What are you doing?" she yelled, before marching to the kitchen. "Mom, why is Mr. Lo in my room?"

"What?" replied her mother. "What's the matter?"

Mr. Lo was a family friend who had helped Amy's mother get her job at the bank. Amy had never heard of him before moving to Hong Kong.

"Did you tell Mr. Lo he could go to my room?"

"Yes. He was just taking off his coat."

"No, he wasn't."

They stepped out of the kitchen.

"I'm sorry. I was putting away my coat. My coat."

"No, you weren't," said Amy.

"Amy, get Mr. Lo something to drink. Would you like some tea, Mr. Lo? Sit down and make yourself comfortable. Nathan, can you turn the TV down a little?"

In the kitchen, Amy leaned over to kiss her grandmother Fan.

"What have you done to your hair?" asked her grandmother, in Chinese. "Most girls are plain and try to make themselves beautiful. My granddaughter is beautiful and she tries to make herself ugly." She cackled.

"It's her attitude that's ugly," said Amy's mother.

"She is still the most beautiful one. I know," said grandmother Fan.

"You should behave with respect. This isn't America," said Amy's mother, changing back to English. "Men will appreciate you for the right reasons."

"Mom, he was in my room, sitting on my bed looking at me. Yuck."

"Oh, stop it. Why would he do that?"

"I don't know, ask him," said Amy.

"When's Jordan arriving?"

"I don't know. Soon."

"Why don't you put your hair up? It looks better that way."

"Mom, I don't need to dress up to study biology."

Amy's mother sighed. It didn't seem as if her daughter appreciated how special this boyfriend was. Amy's mother had passed over many young men to find him. Jordan was not only from a family of doctors, but a pre-med student himself, and tall like Amy's maternal grandfather.

"Does Dad know about Mr. Lo?"

"What do you mean? What is there to know? He doesn't have a right to know."

"Forget it," said Amy.

Amy left the kitchen and the conversation switched back to Chinese.

"How old is Lo?" asked grandmother Fan.

"I don't know," said Amy's mother.

"He's never been married?"

"No."

"Why not?"

"I don't know, Mother. I can ask him at dinner."

"It's a bad sign."

"Bad sign. Too many bad signs."

"Have you heard from Mr. Lee? Will he take you back?"

"What are you talking about? Don't speak nonsense."

"You should forgive him."

"You should mind your own business."

The intercom buzzed.

"Amy!"

Amy was at her desk. Her brother was sitting crossways on her bed, leaning against a Shakira poster.

"Dad said he might come over for my birthday."

"Cool," she said, without looking up.

"Amy."

"Yeah."

"Do you think he's going to get married again?"

"What? Oh. I don't think so." Then she mussed his hair. "Don't worry. He'll still be your dad."

"Do you think he'll have more children?"

"Huh? No." Then, under her breath: "He already has too many."

"Amy!" called her mother. "Jordan's here."

"I have to study now. Hey, make sure Mr. Lo doesn't come into my room next time, all right?"

"Yeah, sure," said Nathan. "I'll build a fort across the entrance."

Jordan poked his head inside.

"Nathan! What's up?"

"I'm good," said Nathan. "Today I made a basket from the free-throw line."

"All right!"

Jordan kissed Amy and then brought in a chair. He looked like a young Chow Yun-Fat. Some girls got nervous when he spoke to them.

"So where do you want to start?" he said.

"Can't we talk a little first? Hey, what about your car! What did you get?"

"A Lexus IS."

"A Lexus! Shit."

"It's Matador Red."

"*Olé*. Nice."

"I'll show you later. Okay. Come on," he said. "Where should we start?"

"Well, Mr. Tutor. That's a very good question. Perhaps one of the sciences."

"You are strange."

"Me?" she said playfully. "You're all business. Why can't you act the way you are on Saturdays?"

"Don't be bad."

"What do you mean by 'bad'?"

"You know . . . ," he said. "We can't be like that in here."

"I'm not asking you to rip your clothes off. Just act natural. Why do people think sex is 'bad,' anyway?"

"Don't worry. I like sex," he whispered.

"But it's bad, right?"

His eyes darted to the door and then he leaned over and kissed her on the mouth.

"Oh, baby," she said.

"Hey, guess what," said Jordan.

"What?"

"We can have the apartment all weekend. My parents are going to Beijing."

"A conference?"

"Yeah. Another boring conference."

"What are we going to do? Throw a party?"

"Yeah. Everyone can stay overnight."

"Great. I'll tell my mom I'm staying over."

"She won't mind?!"

"I don't know. It's not like she could do anything. Anyway, she trusts you."

"Why?"

"You're so handsome and mature and you look like her father, apparently. Anyhow, it's not the first time I've spent the night at a boyfriend's house."

42

"What does she think you do?"

"I don't know what she thinks."

Everyone used chopsticks to serve themselves from the dishes in the middle of the table, except Nathan, who preferred to use a fork.

"Jordan is studying medicine at Hong Kong University," said Mrs. Lee.

"Ah," said Mr. Lo.

"Jordan, do you think Amy can go to Hong Kong University?" Mrs. Lee asked. "I know it's very difficult."

"I think she has a good chance if she studies hard."

Amy scoffed.

"I'm going to design clothing," said Amy.

"Don't be silly. Fashion is only a hobby."

"Unbelievable."

Mr. Lo and Jordan ate almost everything. Grandmother Fan ate almost nothing; Amy and her mother grazed. Nathan avoided the vegetable dishes.

"So, do you think Amy is becoming more like other Hong Kong girls?"

"Oh, great," said Amy.

"I'm sorry about her hair," said Mrs. Lee.

"Mom!"

Jordan laughed. "I think she's like Hong Kong girls.

Maybe a little different."

"I think Asian men prefer women to be less aggressive, don't you?" said Mrs. Lee.

"I don't give a shit," Amy mumbled.

Mrs. Lee smiled weakly and shook her head. Then she patted Jordan's hand.

"It's okay. I don't mind," said Jordan.

"What do your parents think of her?"

"They think she is very nice."

"Hello. Can we talk about something else?" said Amy.

"I worry that she's not Chinese enough. We should have taught Amy and Nathan to speak Chinese, but we didn't think they would need it."

"Ah," said Mr. Lo, looking up from his food. "Nathan will learn quickly. He hardly has an accent." Mr. Lo then considered the last prawn.

"Yes, but Amy won't say anything in Chinese," said Mrs. Lee. "Do you ever try to speak to her, Jordan?"

"In Chinese? No." He smiled.

"What about your friends?"

"They all can speak English."

"It is not just language, though," said Mrs. Lee. "Bringing up children is very different in America. There's not enough discipline. Children are very difficult to control."

"Also in Hong Kong," said Mr. Lo.

"Children are taught to be more respectful to their elders

over here. They are taught what is right and wrong."

"I think people know that in San Francisco, too, Mother."

Mrs. Lee shook her head. "American children don't know as much as they think they do."

"I'm not saying I know everything, but some of the Form 6s here are so out of it. They act like little kids. I don't see the point."

Mrs. Lee looked at Jordan. "What do you think of religious education? You belong to a Christian fellowship, yes?"

"Yes. Many people find comfort in Christ during the hard times of study."

"See," Mrs. Lee said to her daughter.

"See what, Mother?"

"I would be happier if my children belonged to such groups." She turned back to Jordan. "You know, my grandfather was a minister. Mrs. Fan's father. Amy is lucky she has you to teach her."

"No," Jordan replied modestly.

Suddenly Mr. Lo made a move toward the last prawn, but Grandmother Fan removed it before he could reach it. She placed it on her granddaughter's plate.

"Jordan's parents are going away this weekend to a medical conference," said Amy.

"They travel so much," said Mrs. Lee, impressed.

"Yes," said Jordan. "It's in Beijing."

"Jordan's having his friends from the Christian fellowship over."

Jordan blushed. "I'm having a small party."

"A party. How nice," said Mrs. Lee. "You have to promise me you'll be very careful."

"Yes, of course," said Jordan, shifting uncomfortably.

"I'm sure your parents have many valuable artworks and china."

That figures, thought Amy.

8

"*Simon, where do you come from?*" asked Leon, who had also been demoted to English class Number Five.

"Kowloon. And you?"

"Kowloon," said Leon, then he switched back to Chinese. "Same old bullshit exercises. We can relax. You watch the NBA last night?"

"Yeah," said Simon, but for once, he didn't want to talk in Chinese. It felt worse than pointless to speak Chinese during English when his oldest friend thought he had betrayed her by not passing and his dream girl could barely say a word in Chinese. Even if passing English was impossible, he hoped to learn a few interesting things to say to Subway

Girl if they ever met again. But the American's class was even dumber than the others.

"Kowloon," said another student. "And what do you like to doing in Hong Kong?"

"I like to shopping. Have you go to Ocean Park?"

"Okay, enough!" shouted Mr. Slaughter. "'Have you ever' questions, like 'Have you ever been to the Grand Canyon?' or 'Have you ever ridden a horse?' are useful when we want to know what people have done in their whole lives. Everyone write down three 'Have you ever' questions and then ask them to your partner."

Long time no C. Nice 2CU, Simon wrote. *Have you ever ridden a horse? Have you ever been to grand canyon? Have you ever failed out of school?*

Thank god for the weekend, thought Amy as she stepped off a minibus and jammed in her earphones. She'd just failed her first math test. Something to do with parabolas and matrices. It was a mystery what all that shit was good for. Still, she had to start paying more attention and stop doodling in her notepad.

"Amy!" She heard someone calling her from across the street.

Sophie and Macy, two of Jordan's friends, were coming out of a Sasa cosmetics shop. University girls.

"We're going to Festival Walk, come with us," said Sophie

in her direct style. Festival Walk was a megamall.

"Okay," said Amy after a moment's hesitation. She liked to hang out with Jordan's friends only when he was around.

"So, do you love him?" asked Sophie as they walked off.

Amy laughed uncomfortably. It was always some inside information that Sophie was after. "Why do you want to know?"

"Many girls like him."

Amy shrugged.

"The girls are jealous of you," Sophie continued.

"They shouldn't be."

As they crossed the street, boys and men stared mostly at Amy. Sophie watched them stare, while Macy looked away. Amy fished in her bag for her half-eaten lunch.

"Every boy is hungry for you."

Amy laughed. "I doubt it. Anyway, I'm taken."

Sophie made a face as they went down the steps to the subway, like she didn't quite believe it.

It was close to rush hour and the underground was packed. On Fridays the station became a meeting place. Halfway down the escalator, Simon heard familiar voices from the platform below. Raymond, Eric, and Steven.

"Do you think she'll say yes?" Raymond asked.

"How do I know?" Steven replied.

"It depends on whether she has a boyfriend, right?"

Simon told himself it would be better to ignore whatever was going on, but he couldn't move away.

Raymond was only too happy to let him know the very latest. "Steven's asking Subway Girl to the graduation party."

"She's here!" Eric said in a loud whisper.

Simon glanced down the platform, half longing to see her, half not wanting her to have such a hold on him. Maybe this time she wouldn't be beautiful. Then he saw her and it was even worse than usual.

"There're three of them."

Steven whistled softly.

Eric whistled loudly.

"Blow job!" Raymond called out from behind his hand.

Amy looked over.

"Blow job!" copied Eric.

Even though they were speaking Chinese, Simon thought she'd get the drift and think he was an idiot too.

"Ask about her friends," Raymond told Steven. "Ask them what they're doing later."

"Ask her if she'll do it with you," said Eric. "Sexy!"

"Sexy!" repeated Raymond from behind his hand.

"Sexy!" said Eric.

"Okay, I'm going," said Steven. Halfway across he noticed Simon walking over too.

"Where are you going, Chan?" said Steven. "Don't you have some bowls to sell?"

Simon didn't reply. He was wondering if Subway Girl was going to remember him.

"Hi," he said in a big voice as he and Steven came up behind them. All three girls turned and stared at Simon, Subway Girl last of all. "Long time no see."

"Yeah," she said after a pause that almost killed him. "How's it going?"

The two older girls just looked him up and down, wondering who the schoolboy was in the outgrown uniform. Then they all got on the train. Steven gestured to the other guys to get on, too.

"Do you go to same school?" asked Simon in English. He didn't want to speak Chinese even when he wasn't speaking to her directly.

The older girls laughed. "No!"

"My mistake," said Simon as the two older girls started whispering in Chinese. Subway Girl finally gave a little smile.

"Your friends are not in high school," said Simon.

"No. They're in university. You think they're beautiful?"

"Uh . . . they're okay."

"You think they're 'sexy,' then?"

"No," he said, and stopped smiling. "I . . . I didn't . . . That wasn't . . ."

"No?" she said, looking straight at him.

Simon shook his head.

"Just your friends think so?"

"Who?"

"Don't worry about it," she told him, and switched back to normal. "You like shopping?"

"No. Not much."

"I do sometimes. That's where we're headed now. I'm kind of in the mood to just sit around and do nothing, though. You know?"

"Yeah, right," said Simon as Steven pushed his way over.

Most of the girls at school thought Simon was good-looking in a clueless way, but Steven was impressive with his slicked-back hair and school blazer.

"Hello," said Steven, in Chinese.

Across the car, the taller girl nudged the prettier one to check out what was going on.

"You know Marc Lee, right?" Steven continued.

"She doesn't speak Chinese," Simon told Steven.

"What?" said Steven, turning back to the hottest girl on the train. "Marc's a friend of mine. He says hi."

She shook her head. "I can't speak Chinese. Sorry."

"What?" said Steven, still in Chinese. "You don't speak Chinese?"

"Isn't she Chinese?" he asked Simon.

"She wasn't born here."

"You speak to her in English?!"

"Yeah."

"I'm sorry," said Steven, in English now. "It's okay, I

speak your language."

"Good for you," she said.

"You can understand Simon?"

"Yeah."

"His English isn't very good."

"It's fine."

"What can you say to her?" he asked Simon, then turned back to Subway Girl. "Where are you from?"

"America."

"America! I have an aunt in America. Where in America?"

"San Francisco."

"San Francisco! That's where my aunt lives! I want to live there. Hey, what are you doing now?" He glanced over at the guys. "Come with us to Tsing Yi. We can talk about San Francisco."

She turned to Simon. "Are you going?"

"No."

"I'm sorry, what's your name?" she said.

"Steven."

"Steven, do you mind leaving us alone now? I'm getting off soon and I just want to finish talking to . . . um . . ."

"Simon, Simon Chan."

"Hi, I'm Amy, nice to meet you." She turned back to Steven. "Okay?"

Steven smiled for a moment, just in case she was joking. "Really?"

Amy nodded. "Uh-huh."

Simon had gone into a trance.

"Was I too mean, Simon?"

He shook his head.

"So, how's your MP3 player?"

"It's okay. Thank you."

The train slowed down.

"Shit, I've gotta get off. Festival Walk. Oh well, it's the weekend, right?"

"Right," said Simon.

"Here, take this," she said, and scribbled something on a scrap of paper. Sophie and Macy were getting off. "Okay. Bye."

"Bye," he said, and looked at the paper. A chat address.

"Throw it out," said Steven, standing behind him again. "She's using you. She tries to make you like her and then she laughs behind your back. I'd just throw it out."

Simon put the paper in his pocket.

9

Seven hours later, there was a line outside the Red Shift club in downtown Hong Kong, otherwise known as Central. The club was cool, located at the foot of the mountains up behind the skyscraper streets. Few students ever went there. Amy was allowed right in. The guys had already gotten a table and were in the middle of a slightly drunk discussion about a Japanese horror movie. Jordan's friends moved over so she could sit beside him.

Jordan was the king. Good at school and good with girls, he knew how to dress up and still look casual, and how to stay the center of attention without ever saying that much.

"How is everyone?" asked Amy.

"Well actually . . . ," said Gary, the guy who spoke the most but had the least experience with girls, "we were very bored before you came, but now we are okay," he said in English. All Hong Kong University students could switch into English quite easily.

"You'll say anything to impress Jordan," said Sophie.

"Yes, of course. Jordan is my master!"

"I thought Tsang Yam-Kuen was your master," said Amy, trying to make a joke.

"Who?" Gary asked.

"You know, the head of Hong Kong." No one had understood Amy's attempt at a Chinese name. She turned red.

"Oh! Oh!" Gary said. "Bow-tie Tsang, Bow-tie Tsang!"

Everyone burst into laughter.

"Haven't you taught her any more Chinese than that?" asked Sophie. "She should find another teacher."

"I'm not her Chinese teacher. Only math and science," said Jordan.

"Which science?"

"Anatomy!" said Gary.

"Maybe she can teach Jordan anatomy," said Sophie, in Chinese, to even more laughter.

"What did she say?" Amy asked Jordan.

"Don't worry."

"No, what?"

"Let's have another drink," said Jordan.

* * *

In the ladies' room, the music thumped and receded as the door opened and shut. Macy clasped Amy's hand as the others were leaving. Macy was pretty but she didn't have much confidence. "Are you going back to Jordan's house?" she asked Amy.

"Uh-huh."

"I think I will come also."

"With Leo?" Leo was the quiet guy with dyed orange hair. He and Macy always sat together.

She nodded.

The door opened again and Macy had to shout. "What will you do there?"

"I don't know," Amy said, laughing. "Why?"

"You will sleep there?"

"Yeah."

"Only sleep?"

"I don't know. Why? Do you need something?"

"For what?" asked Macy.

"I don't know. Protection?"

"No. Will you need?" said Macy, embarrassed.

"Probably."

Macy whispered. "So you have sex with Jordan tonight?"

"Maybe. Yeah."

Macy moved backward. "Really? How many times have you . . . ?"

Amy shrugged. "A couple of times."

"So many!" said Paula.

"No," said Amy.

"I have never. Can you tell me? Will I be painful?"

"Maybe a little," said Amy. "The first time."

"Really? Very painful?"

"Shouldn't be. If he's slow and—"

"It's okay," said Macy. "I'm just interested. That's all. Don't tell anyone."

When they went back out, the DJ had started his set and a deep *bm boom* was vibrating through the bar. She and Jordan headed toward the dancing. It was her favorite part of the night and people didn't look away quickly when they saw her.

10

Amy sat with Jordan in the back of a taxi climbing up Victoria Peak mountain to the Midlevels, where he lived. From the tallest apartments, you could see everything—the city, the harbor, Kowloon, and on a clear day, the mountains of China.

"Are you tired?" Jordan whispered.

"Not at all," she said.

The party got under way in no time. The television went on. The wine was opened. Cigarettes were smoked. Couples paired off.

In Jordan's room, Amy lit a candle and Jordan unzipped

her dress. Then she lifted her hair and Jordan kissed the back of her neck.

"So salty," he said.

"Sorry."

She turned to face him and he put his hands on her shoulders and pulled off her dress. She stood there with her hair down and looked up at him. His blood rushed and he brought her close.

He took off his pants and she felt him against her stomach. She lifted up his shirt and they pulled it off together. Then he took hold of her again and they fell onto the bed and she laughed as they rebounded. When they sat up again, he reached for her bra and unclipped it. Then she leaned toward him and he pushed her back onto the bed.

"Kiss," she whispered as they pressed together. But he arched up and reached down to bring himself into her.

"Wait. Condom."

"Just once without."

"No, we can't."

"Just once. Just see how it feels and then I'll stop."

She murmured a protest as he slowly put himself inside her. He sighed and she kept her sigh to herself. He pushed himself in all the way and he withdrew slowly. Then he did it again. And this time it was easy.

"Do you like?" said Jordan.

"Okay, that's enough," said Amy.

Jordan sighed and continued.

"Get the condom," said Amy and she put her hands against his chest, and he stopped.

"But it feels so good."

"Go," said Amy and she pulled the sheet up.

Jordan leaned over to grab the condom. Then he blew out the candle. Amy could hear him take off the wrapper but she couldn't see him put it on.

"Slow," said Amy.

And slowly he pressed and slowly she took him inside of her. She sighed with pleasure.

"So good," he whispered. And he started to move faster than before, faster than ever before.

"You have the condom on, right?"

"Mmm."

"Jordan?"

"No." And then he sighed louder.

"What?" said Amy. "Get off!" and she raised her knees. But he was heavy and he had to finish. Then he tumbled onto his back beside her and exhaled deeply.

"Whoa," he said and reached for her hand.

"Fuck!" she said, and swatted it away.

"What?" said Jordan, still panting.

"What do you think?! When I say 'get off,' I fucking mean get *off*! Do you understand?" She hit him.

"Calm down," he whispered.

"You came. I can't believe it."

"Don't worry," said Jordan. "It's just one time."

"It only takes one time! You're a medical student. You should fucking know that!"

"But you've done it before and it was okay."

"What? What are you talking about? Not like this, ever!"

"Don't worry," said Jordan.

"Don't worry? It's not you who has to worry!"

He put his hand on her shoulder.

"How could you do this to me?" she said.

"I didn't mean to . . . I just wanted to try one time. It's gonna be okay."

"How do you know?"

11

"Hey, Max, can I log in?" Max was the computer-room monitor as well as fellow English class Number Five student.

"Are you crazy?"

It was the end of lunch. Time to head to class.

"I'll say you didn't know."

Max mumbled a curse and pointed to a screen. "You have to reserve lunchtime as soon as you get to school."

"I forgot," said Simon.

He checked his emails, then his chat list to see if she was there. He'd written her a couple of days earlier at a karaoke party but hadn't heard back. Still nothing.

"Thanks."

Max went over to shut down the computer.

"Are you writing from school or the karaoke bar?"

"Huh?" mumbled Simon.

"Your message," said Max. "It says 'Are you writing from school or the karaoke bar?'"

Simon walked back over. "Whoa." It's her.

Heathrow: School.

The bell sounded for the beginning of the fifth lesson.

"Don't worry, Max. I'll take care of it."

"They will kill you," said Max, as he turned off the lights and shut the door.

One moment the computer had been this dead thing and now it was like a magical portal.

girLee: Same.

Heathrow: So bad.

girLee: Thanks for your message. It was funny.

Heathrow: Is it lunchtime?

girLee: Yeah. What classes do you have next?

Heathrow: English and biology. What do you have?

girLee: I don't know. Something horrible.

Heathrow: Your weekend was good?

There was a pause.

girLee: Terrible. Karaoke sounds much better.

Heathrow: Why so terrible?

Another pause.

girLee: Boyfriend stuff.

He felt bad even though it was dumb to feel bad. He tried to write something quickly but he couldn't think of anything to say.

girLee: Are you trying to think of something interesting to say? I hope you can think of something interesting.

Heathrow: Yes, I'm trying. But I am not successful.

girLee: That's okay. Boring is good. Otherwise I won't be able to go back to class. It'll make it worse. Like eating chocolate after grapefruit. I mean grapefruit after chocolate.

Heathrow: I'm sorry I cannot be so boring.

girLee: It's easy. Don't try so hard.

Heathrow: Do you enjoy karaoke?

girLee: Love.

Heathrow: You are not shy?

girLee: No.

Heathrow: I think it's good thing. Many people are too shy . . . for everything.

Another pause.

girLee: It's probably good to be shy about some things.

Heathrow: I don't think.

girLee: Why?

Heathrow: It is waste time. It is too boring to sit and say nothing or do nothing.

girLee: I agree.

They sent their next lines together.

girLee: What do you mean you've lost interest in everything? You mean school?

Heathrow: Do you like Chinese food?

Heathrow: I don't know.

girLee: I'm Chinese.

girLee: What will you do next year?

It made him lean back from the computer and notice what time it was—ten minutes past the beginning of class. If a teacher found him now it would be bad news.

Heathrow: Hard to say.

girLee: Are you rich?

Heathrow: No.

He heard someone walking along the balcony.

girLee: So what will you do? Get a job?

The footsteps stopped and the door began to open.

girLee: Sorry. I'm too nosy.

A teacher walked in and turned on the light.

"What are you doing in here?"

Simon looked at the teacher and then back at the screen.

"STOP AT ONCE!" the teacher yelled.

12

Five minutes after Amy closed her biology textbook, she couldn't recall which subject she'd been studying or which one she still needed to study. She opened a fashion magazine and couldn't focus on that, either. The dates of her last period and the one to come kept circling in her head. She figured her last one came fourteen or fifteen days before her night with Jordan, which made it the worst time for her to have unprotected sex. Not that there was a good time. But that was when she was supposed to be ovulating. Still, plenty of the stuff had come back out, she remembered. On her legs. On the sheets. She just couldn't wait to put the whole mess behind her. Couldn't wait the ten days or so for the pain to start up again.

She reached underneath her mattress and drank a miniature bottle of vodka and thought about the boy she'd been e-chatting with at lunchtime. So what was wrong with asking people what they were doing next year? She felt like writing him back and asking him what his problem was. He'd just stopped messaging. It was like he'd hung up on her. She switched on her computer.

Speak of the devil.

> Dear Amy,
> I'm sorry to stop talking to you. Students are not allowed to chat in my school. So I must finish when a teacher came into the computer room. If I use messenger at school again they will shoot.

She smiled. Simon, what were you thinking?

> I don't know what is my plan for next year. Maybe just wait to die. What is your plan? Will you go study in university?
> All the best,
> Simon

All the best?

> Hey Simon, you should have told me. So are you reading

this in chains? I didn't know you were risking your life. . . .
It's not worth it. Don't get in trouble, okay?

Why aren't you allowed to chat, anyway? That's a strange
school rule. Schools are strange little countries. You
know? I mean, we have to go through them and you take
the work seriously but everything else is a joke. Last week
this girl was sent home because she wore nail polish. I
mean, who cares? So threatening to school values! If I was
a teacher I'd tell my boys and girls they could do what
they want, think what they want, wear what they want,
and believe what they want as long as they don't hurt
anyone and they do their work. Seriously. That's it! But
schools are these correctional institutions. I used to get
angry, but now . . .

She paused. "Yeah, I'm so peaceful now." She deleted her
last line. Drank another miniature bottle.

Do you ever go into deep trances? I go into deep ones
during assembly and I think one day I won't be able to
come out of one. After the announcements and the slides
and the ceremonies and gifts and the praying and the
speeches, etc., I'll be stuck in a vegetable state. "Wannabe
fashion designer drowns in pool of drool during assembly
in Catholic girls' school."

She started to giggle. "Shhh." Everyone was asleep.

Are you really not going to school next year? How do you
know so early? You'll just have your F5 Certificate then?
Life in F6 isn't that bad you know, despite everything I've
written to this point. And we can talk on the train. Come
on, Simon. If you're not there I'll have to move to the
other end of the platform to get away from your "friends."

To answer your questions, I'm planning to study fashion
design at some school of design maybe if I'm lucky.
There's a pretty famous one in SF. I went to their graduate
fashion show last year and it was wow. . . . It's pretty
tough to get in, though. Anyway, we'll see. It doesn't have
to be in America. It depends on a few things. Sorry I've
babbled on. Okay, bye.

13

"*Okay, students,*" said Mr. Slaughter, "let's do something completely different. For this lesson, I'm going to be an English-language computer."

"Turn off!" said Kenny and Leon.

"Ahh-hahahahaha! So funny!" The Number Fives erupted. Simon, too, even though he'd been in detention every break time for the past two days.

The American went on. "Your job is to tell me a situation where you need English to succeed or to survive, and I will give you the words."

There was a moment's silence, a few calls of "crazy" in

Chinese, and then most of the class returned to their conversations.

Simon guessed someone was supposed to say that you needed English to survive the Leaving Certificate exam. Then, the teacher would torture everyone with a list of exam vocabulary. What else did English teachers teach? There was no way he was answering. He was sure he wouldn't learn anything for the subway, and he wasn't going from an F to a pass in one class . . . or fifty.

He was so sick of school. All he wanted was to be invisible for the remaining weeks, but even that wasn't working out.

The geography teacher who had caught him in the computer room had given him three hours of detention per day until further notice. That lunchtime he'd started lecturing Simon too.

"It is one thing to leave school without a Certificate, but it is even worse to leave school without a good character," the teacher had told him. "Not everyone can be successful, but if you are respectful and hardworking, people will like you. Does anybody like you, Chan? Where are all your friends?"

Simon had felt a little dizzy after that. He started to wonder if he really had turned out bad.

"Surely you can think of something," continued Mr. Slaughter. "How about for a job as a waiter in an international restaurant? Who knows what a waiter is?"

A few students raised their hands.

"I used to make a good salary being a waiter. Do you know what tips are? Extra money someone gives you on top of the bill. So if the bill is one hundred and twenty dollars and they tip you fifteen percent of the bill, how much is that?"

"Eighteen dollars," said Max, Kenny, Karen, Andy, Leon, Cheung Kit Ying, Ivy, and five others.

"Eighteen dollars cash," said the American. "It's not a bad way to make money *and* you can get a waitering job in any country. Improve your English. Meet people. It's great for traveling."

Simon felt for a pen in his bag. All of a sudden it looked like one of his last classes could be useful.

"Talk to a customer," one student directed.

"Too easy," said Leon. "'Can I help you?' 'Here, eat this.'"

"Shhh!" said the rest of the class.

"Okay," said the American. "You say 'Good evening,' or 'Good afternoon,' or 'How are you this evening?'" He then scrawled the phrases on the board.

"How are you this evening?" Simon repeated as he wrote down the words.

"Then you say, 'What would you like to drink?'"

"What would you like to drink?"

"Sometimes you have to remember what the specials are, so you say, 'Today's specials are such and such,' but that's in a formal restaurant. Normally the specials are written on little blackboards."

Simon raised his hand for the first time in thirteen months. "Specials?" he asked.

"That's the food that's not on the normal menu. Does everyone know what a menu is?"

"Of course!"

"After you give them time to look at the menu, you say, 'Can I take your order now?'"

"Can I take your order now?"

"Then when you bring the food you can say, 'Enjoy your meal,' and then smile so you get a bigger tip. 'Enjoy your meal' or 'Bon appétit.' That's French."

"Born appatee."

"Also, you should check your customers while they're eating. 'Is everything okay?' and 'How was that?' as you clear the plates. Then give them a little time and ask, 'Would you like to look at the dessert menu? Coffee? Tea?'"

Simon copied everything down. He hadn't written so much all year.

"Good!" said the teacher. "What else?"

"I need to meet a girl!" Max cried out.

"Yeah!" the boys shouted.

"Where?" asked the teacher.

"In a club!"

"That's not really . . . I'm not sure we should . . ."

"Hey, girl!" shouted one student.

"No, no," said Mr. Slaughter.

"Hello, you are beautiful girl I want to make love!"

The girls screamed with disgust. The boys cheered. Simon chuckled. It was the best English lesson he'd ever had. Then the siren rang and everyone raced out.

Simon walked along the corridor toward the staff room. The geography teacher would be looking for him in thirty seconds. What would their talk be about this time? He'd just gotten over the last one. He looked at the stairs leading out of the school, then back to the staff room, then back to the stairs again. Detention and lecture or stairs and freedom? Prison life or life as a fugitive. Get kicked out or walk out. Fail or drop. Study for nothing or have nothing to do. No future or—

"Chan! Where are you going?!"

"Good-bye, school," he whispered as he rounded the stairwell and plunged toward the back exit.

"CHAN TZE MAN!"

He glanced around for Katie, but he didn't see her. It was better that way, he figured. He half-expected a siren to go off as he jumped through the back gate. Nothing.

In Mongkok, he looked at a few of the latest MP3 players and noticed that even the cheapest ones were more than he could afford, and he wondered what he was going to do now that he was a dropout.

He sat down on a step, carefully unfolded his printout of her email, and read it again. Fashion design was a perfect choice, he thought, though he would have felt the same if she'd planned to teach Chinese. Thinking what he would write back pulled him together. He wasn't going to sound scared to her. He'd say he had plans. He would become a waiter.

14

True to his plans, Simon went to look for work as a waiter the next morning, though he still dressed for school and left at the normal time. His parents might not have asked about leaving school, but they definitely would have asked why he was going to Central to find a waitering job. "What's wrong with the restaurants in Tai Wo Hau?" he could hear them say. "What a crazy idea!" But downtown was where people spoke English.

When he got off the subway he took off his school tie and sweater and walked way up to a cobblestone lane of restaurants and bars where all the signs were in English. Simon liked a place at the top of the lane. It was brighter than the others, with large windows and white tablecloths. He climbed the stairs.

A European man dressed in a suit gave Simon a quick once over.

"What do you want?" he asked.

"Can I be waiter in your restaurant?" Simon said, in English.

"You have experience?"

Simon shook his head.

"I'm sorry, we cannot hire people without experience."

"No?"

"No."

"Oh," said Simon, and he walked back down the stairs.

What have I done? He decided to return to the station quickly. Maybe he could make it to school by the beginning of lunch, say he'd lost his mind.

He glanced at the other restaurants on his way down. They didn't have steamy glass fronts or crispy duck and pork hanging on display. He liked how they were all open to the street. He saw a woman cleaning glasses inside a place called Pierre's.

"Can I be waiter for you?" Simon called out. Now that he didn't think he had a chance of getting a job, it was almost fun asking for one, like shouting into the mountains. "Can I be your waiter?" he shouted again.

"Come back at six!" the woman yelled.

"Me?" Simon asked.

"Of course you," the woman said with annoyance, then disappeared through a swinging door.

"Ai ya ya," Simon whispered.

He studied the chalkboard out front. The writing was all in English as he'd hoped, but there were a lot of foods he hadn't learned the name of. He wrote down *filet mignon*, *paté*, and *mousse*. He hoped they didn't really mean "mouse."

The tables were all square, not big and round like in good Chinese restaurants. There were photographs on the walls too, which was unusual. He could see the word *Paris* written underneath one of the pictures. Interesting, he thought.

When the sky matched the dark gray suits of the people rushing home, Simon returned to Pierre's. He'd called his parents to tell them he'd be home late. He didn't know how late.

The same woman, Olga, was in the restaurant, but this time a guy named Nigel told him what to do. He spoke English really fast.

"Come with me," he said.

They walked around to where the restaurant kept its garbage bins and empty-bottle crates. The cloakroom was filled with belongings and body odor. Simon rested his backpack on the floor. Another European guy was in there combing his hair.

"So your English is okay, is it?" said Nigel.

"Maybe. I hope."

Then a bell sound came from the kitchen.

"Service!" shouted Nigel and rushed back through the swinging doors. Simon followed him through the kitchen and out the front again. Nigel brought out food, then seated customers. Simon held on to the bar counter like he did to the rail at ice rinks.

"Lady," Olga said, placing a glass of champagne on a tray and pointing to a table.

Simon reached for the glass.

"Tray!" said Olga.

Simon picked up the tray with the glass on it. Two steps later, the glass tipped over and crashed to the floor.

Everyone in the restaurant turned to see what had happened. Simon busied himself putting the pieces of glass on his tray. When he finally returned to the bar, Olga was shaking her head with disgust.

"Big mistake," she said.

Simon dreaded getting another champagne glass until he spotted Nigel with one and learned the secret. Instead of putting the glass in the center of the tray, Nigel put it on the edge, which made no sense until he saw Nigel's thumb coming over to pin it down. It led to Simon's first smile of the night.

He was shown where the beer was stored. He carried

back trays of dirty glasses and brought out hot, clean ones. He watched the waiters talking with one another and laughing with customers, and he never said a word himself.

He carried food only once. An order had been waiting under the heating lamps, and Pierre, the chef, was yelling at everyone in sight to take it out. Simon could understand the repeats of "fucking" but not much else. Nigel pointed to two dishes before he loaded up himself and went back into the restaurant. Simon tried to copy the way Nigel covered his arm before he took the hot plates. It wasn't until his way back to the bar that he noticed the sharp pain coming from his forearm and saw the welt mark. He put on a Band-Aid and went back to drinks.

"What's that?" said Nigel at midnight. "Six hours?"

Simon nodded.

"Here," he said and handed him a pay packet. "I took off the price of the champagne."

"Okay."

"I'm only joking." Nigel laughed. "We're not that bad, are we?"

Simon looked inside the envelope. It wasn't a lot, but it was the most he'd ever been paid.

"Now Olga and I have decided . . ." Nigel began.

Simon's heart began to pound. It felt like getting back an

exam. He told himself he didn't want the job anyway.

"We thought you did pretty well and want you to come tomorrow at six."

Yes! Success!

The rest he was too tired to understand or follow. He just nodded, got his bag, and took off slowly down the hill. At the bottom, in the dark and mostly empty streets of Central, he felt alone and a little lost, but more like a man than ever. And as he looked for a bus back to Kowloon, he wondered where she was, probably where the music was playing, in the dark and with older guys.

15

For eight days and nights Simon worked in Central and the only person who seemed impressed about it was himself. Amy hadn't written anything, even though he'd sent her three emails. His parents shook their heads when they heard it wasn't Chinese food. He'd called Katie but she was angry at him for dropping out of school, though she did cut him some slack for saying he'd still go with her to the graduation party.

It wasn't his plan to be working so much. He'd just said yes every time they'd asked him—drinks, dishes, it didn't matter. He had enough money now to buy a decent MP3 player, he just wasn't sure how much he'd use it. He'd gotten accustomed to owning one that didn't work. It was strange having money but not knowing what to spend it on. It seemed like he didn't have any interests.

Amy was tired of being the girl everyone knew had had sex or liked sex or knew about sex. She told Jordan she wanted to cool things off for a while but that she'd still see him at the clubs. This weekend she needed to catch up on her homework and look after her brother.

Sophie called to find out why Amy had left so early the morning after the party. Amy just said she was stressed about school.

She liked Simon's emails even though she hadn't written him back. His letters made her laugh when she was in bad moods, which was often these days. She thought about finally writing Simon, but decided to surprise him at his restaurant instead. Nothing major.

The cobblestone lane was packed with people spilling out of the bars and cafés, drinks in hand. Guys stared at Amy as she passed even though she was only in jeans and a T-shirt—not her usual night look. Simon's restaurant was supposed to have red and white tables and a blonde behind the bar. She saw the tables first and then the woman.

"Does Simon work here?"

"Who?"

"Simon."

"Busy," said Olga.

There was this place up the road. She could hang out there on the roof while he finished. It was a smallish dance club with bizarre decor. He might get a kick out of it. She wrote him a note.

"Could you give this to Simon, please?"

Olga frowned, then stuck her hand out.

Wow, thought Amy. She hoped Olga was nicer to Simon.

Simon was waiting for Nigel to scrape his plates so he could tie up the garbage bag and take it out.

"A girl was asking for you."

"Huh? When?"

"Very cute. Perfect English."

"She's here?" Simon asked as he tore off his apron.

"She's your girlfriend?"

"No."

Olga rolled her eyes when Simon reached the bar. "This is business. You understand?" Then she threw the note on his tray.

Simon, where are you? I'm going to Z Top if you want to come. I like your restaurant! Amy

It had really been her. All the way up there. His restaurant and the whole street felt brighter.

Where was Z Top? he wondered. He guessed it had to be a club. It was already almost eleven. Whoa. He'd never been to a nightclub. He was wearing school pants and an old track top. Would they let him in with what he was wearing? He'd never seen her in normal clothes. He'd never seen her boyfriend, either.

Her note scared him as much as it made him happy.

16

The club was thumping. The bar was biker-gang black vinyl while the rest of the room looked like it came out of Dr. Seuss. Amy loved the beaded lampshades, the fluffy rugs, and the crazy-shaped psychedelic sofas. White shirts and teeth glowed in the ultraviolet light. She had one Manhattan, danced alone, then sat on the roof with the other city watchers. She got scared when she thought she caught a glimpse of Leo, but she figured he wasn't the only person in Hong Kong with that hair color.

Simon got out at a quarter to midnight. Groups of cool-looking people passed him as he neared the thud of music, many of them wet as if they'd just played basketball. He wondered what kind of dance could have produced such a result. Finally he saw a building with moving figures on the roof and guessed it was Z Top. He looked down at his gray pants and school shoes and tried to think of something else. Then the building seemed to call him.

"Simon! Up here!"

Amy ran back inside to find him at the entrance before he got lost in the crowd. But she stopped dead when she saw the face underneath the orange hair. It *was* Leo. "Oh god, Jordan must be here," she said, then looked for the others.

Simon inched his way out of the packed elevator and into a dark hallway. The music was so loud that the bass notes were like small earthquakes. He froze a little when the doors to the club swung open and he was inside the coolest place he'd ever seen. This is what life is about, he told himself. Traveling to interesting places. Then to his relief, he saw her walking in his direction, but she was looking everywhere except at him.

"Amy!"

He thought hearing her name scared her, but she seemed happy enough when she saw it was him.

"You came. Cool." Then she looked over her shoulder again. He'd never seen her distracted like this. "How are you?" she said. "It's been ages."

"It's great place!" he said.

"Yeah. I love it too. All the colors."

She seemed to hear someone call her again.

"Did you lose your friends?" he asked.

"No, no. I was just . . ." She didn't know what to tell him. "I thought I saw a guy I know."

"Oh," he said, like it was to be expected. "It's okay. I can . . ." He looked around for something he could do. She watched him search inside his pockets and didn't know whether to touch his hand and start again or hug him good-bye. She liked that he was wearing clothes from work.

"Do you want to dance?" he heard himself say.

"Um . . ."

"You don't have to," he said.

"You like dancing?" she asked. "Most of the guys I know don't like to."

"Yeah," he lied.

"Okay, come on," she said. Screw them, she thought. "Let's have one dance."

Her body was like liquid, moving slow and easy to the music, and he was like hard noodles, stiff but trying to jiggle. Still, it was the greatest. I'm dancing with her, he thought. And as the wordless song continued on and on, he started to feel a bond with all the other dancers and with all nightclubs and with people everywhere.

Then a guy who looked like a young Chow Yun-Fat started dancing behind Amy, or not dancing so much as imitating her, but all quick and violent. At first she didn't notice, but then she did.

"Jordan, what are you doing?!"

"You didn't think I would be here?"

"I don't care. I'm just dancing. Look, can you leave me alone, please?"

"Come on," he said.

"What do you mean? Where?"

Her boyfriend, thought Simon. It made sense. They spoke to each other very passionately. It made him remember a movie where the hero said that it was only true passion when it hurt. And then he watched Jordan grab her arm and he forgot about movies.

"Leave her alone," he said in Chinese.

"What?" said Jordan, turning around. "You. Fuck off." Then he pulled Amy toward him.

"We're leaving!" he shouted at her.

"What are you talking about?" Amy said. "Stop it. I'm not with you."

Jordan grabbed her shoulders and started shaking her.

"Take your hands off her!" Simon yelled.

"Who is this piece of shit?" said Jordan.

"You're a piece of shit," Simon said. "Leave her alone. She doesn't want to see you."

Jordan laughed. "Didn't I tell you to fuck off? Come on," he told Amy, and started to drag her out.

"Let me go. You're hurting me."

Simon had never been in a fight before, but he flew at Jordan to pry him off her. But Jordan swung free with his elbows and caught Simon in the eye. Simon turned his head away but managed to keep Jordan from going after her.

When Amy saw Simon's eye, she went wild, kicking Jordan in the stomach and knocking him back into Leo and the others.

The dance floor was spread out now so people could watch the fight, but the two parties had separated for good. Amy turned away and Jordan stood up again with his friends in the background.

"Fucking whore!" he yelled out in English, still doubled over. A few girls gasped. Amy wondered if Simon understood the word. Part of her wanted to go back to Jordan and finish him off.

"We can go now," said Simon.

"Oh shit," Amy said when she saw his eye again.

"It's okay."

"Let me get some ice."

"No, it's fine."

"I'm sorry about this," she said as they walked out. "That was my boyfriend. *Ex*-boyfriend."

17

"I don't like that boy shit, you know? It's so pathetic." She aped boxing. A couple of minibuses passed them, then a couple of taxis. Otherwise, the streets of Central were quiet. "You're not like that, are you, Simon?"

"I don't know."

"You were great, though. Thank you."

"It was easy. I'm black belt."

"Let me see that," she said, looking at his eye. "Ouch. I think it might have stopped swelling at least. Can you see?"

"Yeah. It's fine."

She smiled. "No, it's not. But it will be. Where are we going, by the way?"

"I don't know."

"I don't know either. I'm just following you, Hong Kong boy."

He pointed to the harbor.

"Anywhere's okay. As long as we can sit down."

He found a bench near the water and she rested against his shoulder. He felt her tug his arm closer and then she was still.

After a time, he felt her stir again. Then, she lifted her head back up and found bits of hair stuck to her face. He glanced at her pulling strands from her mouth and chin.

"How embarrassing. Uh-oh," she said, when she noticed his eye.

"It's okay. I can see."

"Yeah, that's the main thing, I guess."

He nodded.

"Looks aren't really important," she added, trying unsuccessfully not to snort.

Then they both broke out laughing.

"Also your hair!" he said. "So interesting."

Then Amy began to laugh less and she ducked her head a little to let her hair tumble and quickly ran her fingers through it. Then he noticed she wasn't laughing anymore, and more than anything, he wanted to kiss her.

So he leaned over, but she lifted up her head at the same time, and they collided.

Amy looked up as Simon brought the back of his hand to his mouth.

"Did you . . . ? Oh no," she said, and burst into giggles. Then she fussed, bringing her fingers close to his lip. "You should have warned me, um . . . well . . . no, not really. Oh, shit. It hasn't been a good night really, has it? Um . . . oh, geez. I'm sorry. Oh, damn it."

He didn't understand exactly what she was talking about, but he feared that he'd made a mistake and she was just trying to make light of it.

She saw the doubt in his eyes and stopped smiling.

Then she leaned over and kissed him. First his top lip, then his bottom lip, and then both together. And their faces stayed close and she smiled, and he thought it was the best thing that could possibly happen to a guy.

Then they kissed again and she liked the way he smelled and his soft lips, even though he was new to it all.

"That tickles," she said, and giggled.

She didn't ever hang out with schoolboys, let alone hook up with them, but here she was.

She wanted to lick his ear but thought it might scare him, or on the other hand not scare him at all, which could spoil things too.

Was she drunk? She didn't think so. She thought about him on the train, making her laugh in English, and wondered if she could she tell a joke in Chinese. No friggin' way.

She'd sound like an idiot. But he wasn't an idiot at all. He was smart, if not maybe in the school way. But she wasn't sure she respected that kind of smartness anyway. The funny thing was, it was she who was the schoolkid now anyway. He was the one working out in the world while she was still wearing her little schoolgirl dress with her little schoolgirl socks. Just an innocent little schoolgirl.

Then she thought of all the things that made her anything but a little schoolgirl, and her missing period came to mind. Goddamn it, Jordan. You fucking . . . But she blamed herself too. Then she took hold of Simon's arm again and fell sound asleep.

18

Black and purple hair poked out of the top of a quilt. The room smelled of cigarettes. Sometimes Mrs. Lee put the smoky clothes on the balcony before her daughter woke up. But there they were, on the chair and on the desk. Nathan inspected her shoes too. The inner label was faded and torn.

"Ayyymeee," he said in his lowest voice. "Ayyymeee."

She stirred.

"Amy," he continued, quick and sharp.

When she opened her eyes, her brother was four inches from her face.

"Nathan. Go away," she mumbled. "Or I'll punch you."

"You wouldn't," he replied. But he climbed off her bed. "Wake up! It's late."

It was park time.

"All right! I'll be ready in a minute."

She grimaced as she slowly rose. Then felt a bit queasy. Then smiled. Maybe it had come. Please. Please.

Still, she opened her desk drawer and took out the pregnancy test she'd bought. Even one day over was too much to bear. She had to know.

She hid the plastic tube against the elastic of her pajama bottoms. Then she walked to the bathroom.

It wasn't difficult to do. You had to pee on a strip and wait to see what came up. If the middle area dried white you were okay, but if it came up dark, you were pregnant. Amy wet it and placed it in her desk drawer when she returned to her room.

"It's Jordan!" yelled Nathan.

"What are you talking about?"

But Jordan was already at her door. "Amy."

She slammed the drawer shut. "Jordan! What are you doing here?"

"I came to say sorry."

She waved and pointed to her mother's room.

"I just want to tell you," Jordan whispered, "it's my fault. I was too drunk. I'm sorry."

Amy moved past him to shut her door. "I don't care anymore."

"I'm sorry. Okay?" He looked at her with big eyes.

"No. Not okay. I don't act like that when I'm drunk. It's just an excuse."

"But I didn't mean it."

"But you did it. I don't like the way you treat me. I don't want to go out with you anymore."

Jordan smiled, but his voice became flat.

"It's that guy, isn't it?"

She blushed slightly.

"Where did you go with him? What did you do?"

"I fell asleep. Look, I don't have to tell you anything."

"Were you seeing him when we were going out?"

"I'm not seeing him. I'm not seeing anyone! Including you."

"You're a sleaze."

"See ya," she said, and turned away.

"I'm not coming back."

"Good."

"Everyone thinks you're—"

"Everyone can think what they want!" Amy shouted.

"So you don't deny it?"

"Deny what? Just go!"

Jordan gave her a look of disgust, then strode out.

One minute later, Mrs. Lee walked into her daughter's room.

"What?!"

"Who is this other boy?"

Oh great, thought Amy. "I hate this place!"

"Where were you last night? Why is Jordan so upset?"

"I went dancing and then I walked around, all right? Where do you think I went? And what's so good about Jordan? What do you think he does when I go over to his house? Shows me his Bible?"

"You cannot behave like this!"

"Like what?"

Mrs. Lee frowned and shook her head.

"Are you going to call me a sleaze too? You're all the same. So holy. So full of it. You think Mr. Lo comes here for your cooking? When are you going to let him in *your* bedroom?"

Mrs. Lee inhaled sharply, then slapped her daughter across the face.

"I hate you!" said Amy, and slammed her door. She steadied herself on the back of her chair. Her head was spinning. Everything felt out of control. Then she looked at her drawer and got a terrible feeling things were about to get a lot worse. It can't be, she told herself. She really needed this not to happen. Maybe she didn't deserve the luck, but please, no. She opened the drawer and saw the color trapped between the lines. "Yup," she said, her chest tight. "Oh god." She began to cry.

19

Mr. Chan's *Golden Oldies* CD came out every Sunday morning. Simon rolled over to put his pillow over his head. Then it all started to come back. What? No. Oh my god. Ha-ha! Unbelievable! He stretched his arms out to welcome the morning, and his left hand smashed against the wall, but he didn't care.

"San Fraaan . . . sisco-o-oh!" he sang. *"Up on a he-e-el, it cawl to me-e-e."* He'd almost gotten into a fight, too. "Listen to me," he told his room. "Don't you ever touch her. Ever. You touch her again and I'll kill you. You understand? Okay. That's all I wanna say."

Mr. Chan was reading the Happy Valley horse racing

guide. Mrs. Chan was looking at the front section of the newspaper and commenting on everything she saw. Mr. Chan wasn't expected to respond and didn't.

"Good morning," said Simon in English.

"What is he talking about?" said Mrs. Chan.

He carried out his bowl of breakfast in one hand and swayed to the music.

"Crazy," said Mrs. Chan. Then she saw his face.

"Ahh. What happened to your eye and your lip?"

"It was an accident. It doesn't hurt."

"Accident," scoffed Mrs. Chan. "Eye and mouth. Two accidents. Go. Get ice," she told her husband.

"Okay, okay," said Mr. Chan, smiling for once. "She was a good-looker?"

"Yes," said Simon.

Mr. Chan chuckled while his wife swore under her breath. Then they all laughed together. Simon wished it was always like that.

That afternoon at Pierre's, cleaning lettuce heads and scrubbing potatoes was almost fun. It was like there was music playing underneath everything he did. After the lunch service, he found an arcade with a tiny internet café and tried to write her a note. But it was harder than he expected. He tried to think in Chinese and then translate into English but it was just as bad. I *uh it uh you uh uh*.

He finally got something out when it was time to go back to work.

> Hi, I'm at work today but I feel very good. My eye has many colors. But no problem. Just I have little strange appearance. How about you? Are you studying today? Yesterday was the great night. Thank you for inviting me. Ha-ha. Simon

It wasn't until Wednesday that he received a reply. He printed it out at the internet café, then waited till he was alone in the back of the restaurant to open it. When he took the paper out of his jacket pocket, he felt butterflies in his stomach. The paper tingled.

> I don't know what I was thinking. So soon after this thing with Jordan. It was stupid of me. I'm not really ready for anything now. Anyway, blah blah blah. Thank you for sticking up for me. I mean it! I'll never forget it. How's your eye, by the way? Are you okay to work? Tell me how it's going with the new job when you have time. I have to get into studying big-time. I'm so behind! Mock exams this week. Back to math now ☹ . . . Amy

He read it through again, hoping he'd missed something.

20

Amy went to an internet café in Mongkok. She wasn't going to research abortion at her school. After an hour she'd gotten nowhere. She'd found "Methods for Termination," "Safety of Termination," "Believers Against Child Killing," and "Postoperative Side Effects and Complications," but no names, numbers, or addresses. The windows were changing too slowly. She started to panic. Finally, she found something promising: "Youth Healthcare Centres." She clicked.

It turned out there was one in Mongkok, another reason for loving Mongkok. She knew the street. They offered an abortion counseling service, a pelvic examination, and a pregnancy test.

She took a break and checked her email. Nothing. She supposed she wouldn't have replied either if he'd sent her an email like the one she'd sent to him. She hadn't wanted any guy coming near her again. But still. She thought about sending him a little message just so he'd have to reply, but she couldn't think of anything interesting to tell him. She just wanted to hear him talk to her. About anything. Make her feel like she was the same.

She headed to Mongkok. Alone. The walk was miserable. It reminded her of the sooty street her mother had dragged them along, just a couple of days after they arrived. Amy was still furious about the move to Hong Kong and Nathan inconsolable, but Mrs. Lee insisted on showing them the Kowloon Flower Market. The smell from the buckets of red and white and yellow and pink and purple and lavender and blue flowers had come up to greet them, and the paper lanterns had all been lit. Her mother had told Amy about it when she was a little girl, how Mrs. Lee used to go there with her mother. It became the first thing Amy loved about Hong Kong.

She stifled a sob. *I'm sorry, Mom.* Then she imagined hearing her mother's voice.

How could you? I trusted you. This is the worst thing you could do to me. You must tell Jordan.

He tricked me, she wanted to tell her. *And then he wouldn't stop.*

But her mother's voice got lost in the noise and Amy started to cry as the buses roared past. She could never tell her mother what had happened. She'd done exactly what she'd been told not to, and she deserved to go through it alone.

Stop crying! You can't be crying in the clinic, she told herself. She had to convince the doctors she was mature enough to know what she was doing.

She put in her earphones for the final blocks and made a mental note not to wear them in the waiting room.

People were supposed to make appointments in advance but there was a cancellation at five. She took a wall seat. She forgot to ask whether it was a woman doctor. It seemed like it would be the type of place where there'd be a lot of women doctors, but she saw only one. She dozed in and out for two hours and wore on her cheek the imprint of her coat's zipper when her name was finally called. It was a man. She snapped to attention then realized she hadn't figured out what she was going to say.

"I . . . I need to get an abortion," Amy began in English.

"Yes, but first let's make sure you're pregnant," replied the doctor, also in perfect English, to Amy's relief.

"It's just that I can't have a baby now, and be a mother. Because, um . . ." She looked at the doctor. "Um . . . I don't know . . . there are things I want to do. I don't know what, but . . . maybe I can't do them if I have a baby now, in high school." It was the first time she'd said any of it out loud, and it choked her up.

The doctor waited for her to look up again. "It's okay, take your time."

She nodded. "Thanks. So. Um. That's . . ." Her mind went blank. "Oh, and . . . the guy, who got me pregnant, we're not . . . we're not close. Now. I mean, we were. He was my boyfriend. It's not like . . . he didn't force me, but I thought he was wearing a condom and he said he was and when I realized he wasn't . . . We've broken up. He has nothing to do with this."

"He doesn't know?"

"No. But I might have to tell him because I think I'll need some help with paying for it."

"You haven't told your mother."

Amy shook her head. "No. I don't want to."

"You are sure?"

"Yes."

Being examined was uncomfortable, but at least it was quick.

She was around four weeks pregnant, which confused her until she learned it was counted from the beginning of the last period. Anything under twelve weeks was considered safe but the earlier it was done, the better. She'd need to go in for one more evaluation but the doctor said they could book her abortion for the following Saturday, the fourteenth.

"Does anyone ever die?"

"The chances of dying due to termination of an early pregnancy are one in one hundred thousand in a hospital or clinc," the doctor said.

So you can die, thought Amy.

The doctor handed Amy an information sheet.

"Can you still have children no problem . . . afterward?"

"Yes. If there was no problem to begin with." He pointed to a diagram on his desk. "We insert a suction tube into the uterus and then we scrape a little and remove the gestational products."

"Sorry? What products?"

"The fetus."

Amy took a deep breath and nodded.

"How long does it take?"

"You can go home that day. Of course, no strenuous activities for a few days," said the doctor. "And no sex for two weeks."

Don't worry, thought Amy.

It cost more money than she had. She walked around for an hour trying to figure out what she was going to do. She didn't want to ask Jordan for anything, but she needed to ask him to pay half. The only thing she was worried about was him telling someone. But she didn't think it was something he'd want other people to know. She didn't worry about him wanting to have the baby.

"We need to talk."

"Yeah? What about?"

Amy bit her lip. She didn't want to start yelling and have him hang up, but his tone of voice ignited her. "Remember when you told me you were wearing a condom when you weren't?"

"So?"

"You know, 'Don't make a big deal about it'? I'm pregnant."

There was a long silence.

"Hello?"

"You're sure."

"I went to the doctor."

Another silence.

"How do I know it's mine?'

"What?! You know it is!"

"How do I know?"

"I'm four weeks pregnant, okay! Look, I just need you to help pay for an abortion."

He made a sound to show he expected as much. "Does your mother know?"

Amy's heart skipped a beat. "No. And she isn't going to."

He laughed. "Of course. She thinks you are a good girl."

"Get fucked," she said and hung up. A minute later she redialed. He didn't answer. His father did. It was a nightmare.

"Can I speak to Jordan, please?"

"Who is speaking, please?"

"Amy." It was the first time she'd felt bad about telling someone her name. Jordan picked up the phone again.

"What?"

She told him how much it was going to cost. He told her how much he'd give her, and then he hung up.

She replaced the phone and broke down. She felt like everything he thought of her. Dirty. Cheap. Used.

When she got home, her aunt Lucy was there for dinner. All her aunt noticed was that the purple in Amy's hair had almost grown out.

"She wants to look nice," said Mrs. Lee. "Her father is coming for Nathan's birthday."

No way.

In her room, Amy leaned against her door and closed her eyes. She'd forgotten. It was just dumb luck the doctor hadn't booked her abortion on her father's visit. Nathan's birthday party was the Saturday after she was going in. A week would be just enough time to recover, she thought, before her attendance was required. She'd tell her mother she had cramps if it came to that. Her father never paid attention to her anyway.

21

About a week after Simon had received Amy's letter, he got a phone call at work.

"Hello?"

The reply came back in Chinese. He was disappointed to hear his own language.

"I don't think I can even get the pass grade," said Katie. "I've heard that the exam is going to be harder this year than usual."

"Don't worry so much. You're the most prepared person I've ever met."

Katie started to sob. "Simon, I always feel like crying. I can't stop worrying."

"Don't worry, Katie. I think everyone is very nervous. Hey, how's your shoebox? How many words do you have now?"

"Six hundred vocabulary cards. Do you still have yours?" she asked.

Simon wiped some crumbs from the bar counter. "Yeah, I think."

"I liked yours better," Katie said. "The airplanes were cool."

"Yeah," he mumbled. He'd forgotten about the 747s and the Antonov An-22. He'd glued them to the sides of his box.

"You're still coming to the graduation party with me, right?"

"Of course."

"I just want to go together, so we can finish school like we started and make jokes about everyone else!"

"Yeah. Good idea."

"Oh, my bus! Is everything okay with you? Are you rich?"

"No."

"It's good to be a waiter?"

"Yeah, but . . ." The line cut out. *I'm not a waiter.* He replaced the phone and went out back to grab his bag from the changing room.

All he was doing was taking out drinks and cleaning dishes. He wondered if he should look for another restaurant job or talk to his parents about working in the shop. It was good, in a way, how they got over his failings so easily. They never even asked him about school and why he wasn't going anymore.

He looked for something to kick. He noted the concrete yard, the wooden stairs, the metal fence, the shed with precariously stacked shelves.

"Hey," called the pastry chef. "Pierre wants you to come back at five thirty."

Simon looked to see if there was anyone else the guy might have been talking to. There wasn't.

"Okay," he replied.

He walked to Queen's Road and stepped into a minimarket. He felt the cool air from the freezer section as he read over his one last email to Amy.

> Hi, Amy. How is everything? I had interesting morning. The chef shout at me but I think he likes to shout for everyone. It was my time to be shout by him. I will go back later. Now I have free time before lunch. So I'm in Central now. How is your study? Are you still behind? It's very easy to fall behind. You think everything is okay and then one day you can't see your classmates. Hello, I'm over here! But they can't see you.
>
> Also your teacher doesn't ask you to answer questions and that's relax but bad for your future. So be careful. But I think you don't need to worry. Because maybe

the people who are worry don't need to worry and the people who don't worry need to worry. So if you worry then maybe you don't need to worry. So maybe I think you should worry but just a little bit. So I think you will pass everything. Okay, take care.

He wasn't sure if he sounded smart or insane. He would read it one more time in the internet café and then maybe send it to her. She'd see that he was fine, and that she didn't have to worry about anything with him. He understood everything. He bought a cold drink and a packet of dried seaweed.

Beside the computer, he flattened his notepaper, then began to copy. *Hi, Amy,* he wrote, then looked back at his notes and flattened them some more. A week ago they'd kissed and now he couldn't even write an email. He looked at the *Okay, take care* and shook his head. Then his heart began to race.

I wrote a letter this morning to you but it doesn't say how I want to say. It's just blah blah blah, you know? I can't write like that to you. I want to send nothing or something but not blah blah.

How are you? I'm okay. Today is a shit day but it's okay now. Soon I'll go back to work. I miss you. I think about you too much. I try to change my mind. You think it was stupid on Saturday. I think it was opposite of stupid. It was the best for me. I still feel you next to me. I can't forget. I try to forget. I don't want to speak. I want to speak. I want to say everything. I don't know how to say. I understand you can't feel this way. Too soon for you. Too soon for me to forget your kiss!

"Yes," he whispered.

I felt everything great but I didn't say anything because I was just want to hold you and I thought I have so much time. I see your eyes and I look out to the sea and I see everything in the world.

Exactly! he thought.

It's okay if you can't feel like this, but I want you to know. Because when you say write when I have time I don't think you know. Maybe you have many times like this and so easy for you to forget. But not for me. I never. I can't forget. I never forget.

Then his eyes went blurry.

I just want to go to the water again with you. But I understand if you don't want to. Don't worry. I'm not like

your boyfriend. I have a job. I take care of myself. Today
is the shit day and I want to speak to someone about
life and I think how can I say my thoughts in English! So
crazy for me. But I just only want to talk to you. That is all
I can say.

Yes! he thought. Finally. She would know everything
now. He dragged the arrow toward Send. But he couldn't
click. No girl, he thought, would want a guy to spill his guts
like that.

22

Discarded flyers blew along the sidewalk under a heavy sky. A storm was coming. Simon was in Mongkok on his way to work. He needed pants that weren't jeans for the graduation party. He was trying to take his mind off Amy, but it was hard. He ended up with a new orange shirt. Then it began to pour.

He ran down the street toward a small subway entrance. He could see it popping out of the road like a submarine hatch. He didn't stop until he reached its first landing, then pressed against the wall as the rain cascaded down. Only the backs of his knees and the contents of his shopping bag were still dry.

As usual, he saw someone who looked like Amy. She was coming down the metal stairwell, hair wet and schoolbag dripping.

Then with a start, he realized it was her.

When Amy saw Simon, she tensed up. He waved and waited for her at the back of the landing. They didn't touch when she got there.

"Damn rain," she said, squeezing the water out of her hair. She was at least as wet as he was, her hair shiny and black. Her beauty frightened him a little. "I tried to run for it, like an idiot. I hope I didn't ruin my earphones."

"Yeah."

"I couldn't be bothered waiting."

He looked at his wet clothes and smiled. "Also."

"I guess it's only water."

They looked at each other and then spoke at the same time.

"Are you going to work?"

"You finish your exam?"

"Yeah, I just finished math," she said.

"Yeah. Work," said Simon. "Math was good?"

"Not really. I don't want to think about it."

"Oh."

Then she took out her sweater and gave his face a wipe before she used it on herself. It was only a little smoother than steel wool and it smelled like the bottom of a schoolbag, but it was her touch and he was a goner all over again.

He looked toward the station, wondering if he should go.

"You're going to be late?" she asked.

"Uh . . ."

"I'll walk you down," she said, and reentered the line before he could argue. They stopped before the turnstiles.

"Do you always get on at this station?" she asked.

"No. I had to buy something." He raised his shopping bag.

"I'm sorry about that email."

"No, I understand. You have to study."

"So everything's going okay with your restaurant?"

"So-so." He shrugged. "What about you?"

"So-so."

"Everything so-so."

"Used to be interesting. Now so-so."

Simon laughed.

"Oh well," she said. "You're not going to be late, are you?"

"No, it's okay," he replied, then looked at the station clocks.

"No, you're lying. I can see. Go."

He tried to smile. "Yeah."

"Will you email me again if I write back? I suck, I know, but . . ."

"I'll email you tonight."

"Really? Great. Have a good day at work."

"You too."

"Bye, Simon."

"Bye," he said, and moved toward the turnstiles.

Amy stayed where she was. She didn't know where she wanted to go. The only person she felt like speaking to had his own life to worry about. Her eyes started to fill. Grow up, she thought, and invented something to look for in her bag as the rough moments passed.

"Did you lose something?" asked Simon. He'd turned back to see the last of her and saw her standing there.

"Huh? Oh," she said without looking up, "I was just . . ."

"Do you need anything?"

She shook her head. "I'm just havin' a bad day," she said in a small voice.

"Don't worry." He couldn't think of anything else to say, but he reached out with his hand and when he did, she leaned toward him. Then he put his arms around her.

When she looked up her eyes were wet but she was smiling. "Well," she said and clutched her bag. "Now you're gonna be late."

"It's okay," he said, and shrugged. "I don't mind."

"Won't you . . ."

"I don't care."

"No?"

He shook his head.

"Do you want to just go somewhere? Just run away?"
"Yes," he said.
"Are you sure? I mean . . . don't lose your job."
"It's bad job."
"Still, it's . . ."
He took hold of her bag and started walking.
"Woohoo!" she shouted. "Where to?"

23

They came out the back of Central station and crossed the last highway, and then it became difficult to see. The fog was thick and the air was wet and salty. Only the hull of an ancient port building stood between them and the sea. As soon as Simon had called his job, they ran to the ferry gates and boarded the first one leaving.

"What did you say?" Amy asked as they ran over the bouncing planks.

"'Hi, I cannot work today.'"

"What did they say?"

"Just hang up."

The boat started to move and Amy giggled and swore as

she bumped into the sides of the stairwell.

On the lower deck, they felt the spray from the motor and watched as Hong Kong came into view. The island looked like what a child would draw. There were lush green mountains, space-age skyscrapers, and the water, all on one page. The ferry headed west, then turned into the South China Sea. They passed stationary barges and saw container ships slide by. Then after a while, the sky began to lighten.

Floating around in the middle of the world, Amy remembered how she wanted to be, and it wasn't being scared. There were so many things she wanted to do. So many things she loved. And yet everything had seemed so dark lately, like she'd ruined her life and that was it. But how could that be it? Not when the world was so big and she felt so alive. It wasn't the end for her or for Simon! She wouldn't let it be.

"No!" she cried as a large wave slapped against the boat and splashed them from head to toe.

Downstairs, an old man was smoking a cigarette next to his live seafood. Simon asked him where they were going. The old man said two words and nothing more.

"Cheng Chau," said Simon.

"Jung what?" said Amy.

"Cheng Chau," he repeated slowly.

"Where's that?" she smiled.

"South."

"South? How can you tell?"

"Kowloon is North."

"Oh, yeah. . . . See, I just listen to my iPod. I don't really pay attention. What's going to be there?"

He pointed at the crates of seafood.

"Seafood restaurants."

"What else?" she asked.

"Water. Some houses . . ."

"Uh-huh."

"Music . . ."

"Good. What kind?"

"Maybe traditional kind."

"Oh."

"Beer," he added just for the hell of it.

"Cool!" she said. "I'll have to camouflage my uniform, though." She was wearing her school's white summer dress. "Maybe you'll have to buy."

"Yeah," said Simon, slightly worried now.

Amy looked back over at the old man. "I think I'll ask him how far."

"Good idea."

No way he understands English, thought Amy as she approached.

"Excuse me. How far are we . . . How much longer to Cheng Chau?"

At first the man didn't seem to have heard, then he slowly

turned his head and pointed to the other side of the boat. There was a hill.

"Oh god." She laughed. "How embarrassing. Thanks. Hey, Simon. We're here."

There wasn't any beach, just a concrete retainer separating the water from the village. Junks and rowboats parked up against it. No cars. No apartment towers. The hills were dotted with brightly colored cottages. They'd never seen anything like it.

Simon glanced at Polaroids of bedrooms, which were displayed outside the first few houses like menus. He wondered what it would be like to stay in one with her. To go to dinner together. Go shopping. Go home. Get changed.

"Wouldn't you like to just stay here?" she said.

"Yeah, why not," he said, acting like the question hadn't blown up his teenage mind.

He followed her into one of the shops.

"What do you think?" she asked, wearing new sunglasses and holding up a dress.

It was like he'd died and come back as someone famous. He'd never been a guy with a girl before. And now he was *her* guy?

"Perfect!"

The restaurants kept their seafood outside, some crowded in large buckets, some swimming around in glass tanks. Crabs. Lobsters. Fish. Prawns. Mussels and clams. The tables overlooked the bay.

"Eat here?" she asked.

He'd never thought about fresh seafood. He'd always had his frozen, dried, and fried, except at his aunt's wedding. It had been okay. To Amy, everything looked familiar and delicious. She was used to going out to restaurants and having her father buy the most expensive dishes. She walked over to the tanks, then checked out the menu. Everything was more expensive than she thought.

"Let's keep walking," she said. "Come on."

Simon asked a waiter how much the fish was that she'd been looking at. How great it would be to buy it for her, he thought. *Yes, we'll have a couple of those, and beer. Thank you. Here, I'll pour that. Wine, too? Sure. Why not?* He pictured everything as she walked ahead and the waiter told him the price.

"Thanks. Maybe later."

Unbelievable, thought Simon. For fish! All you have to do is pick them out of the water. *Give me a stick.* He'd have to figure out some other place to take her. He had cash, but he wasn't a millionaire.

"So, do you really think you could live here?" she asked him.

"Maybe. What about you?"

"I think I could for a while, especially at the moment.

I think it would get a little boring, though."

She closed her eyes and felt the sun on her face. They were sitting along one of the retainer walls.

"You sort of live on an island anyway when you go to school," she said. "A desert island. It's . . . What do you call those guys in the orange shawls? You know . . . ah, what are they called . . . bald . . ." She pressed her hands together as if she were praying.

"Yeah . . . um . . ." He didn't know how to say "monk" in English.

"I mean that's what they want you to do. Just study and pray. But how does that make you the best person?" She shook her head.

Simon smiled.

"The university students I know aren't that smart, in some ways."

"Really?"

"Yeah. Just studying for hours—for years—out of textbooks. Most of it only for an exam. Just filling your head with . . . I don't know what it is. . . . Might as well read telephone books. I mean my class is full of geniuses—well, school geniuses—but . . . We're given this discussion topic about which guest speaker to invite to our school and there's this list with a gay doctor on it, and a philosopher, a woman judge, an African chief, and some others. So immediately almost everyone crosses out the doc and

I'm like, why? He's gay, so case closed."

"I think we had that same discussion," said Simon, recalling a painful memory though his class had a shorter list.

"Yeah. Oral exam shit. I don't remember many of my lessons but I remember that one. I've got a shit memory. I've been trying to write more things down lately. Not sure it's working. I think I'm going to fail."

"I can't believe."

"Really. I mean, I hope not. I want to pass. For design school. I don't care about anything else."

Simon nodded. It was a smart way to be.

"I know you're different," she added. "You just couldn't stand it any longer. But you could still pass if you did the exams, right?"

"No," he said.

"What do you mean, no?"

"I write wrong answers."

Amy laughed. "Me too. School makes you stupid, doesn't it? Which is recommended for girls, actually . . . kind of." She paused for a moment as if considering whether to bring something up. "We had this sex education class, just one, and the teacher's obviously . . . well, she . . . I don't think she's ever had sex and so anyway all she does is point to this diagram like, 'This is the penis and this is the uterus,' and everyone's, like, hysterical. 'Wow, look!' It was so dumb. Yeah . . . Oh well," she shrugged, a little embarrassed.

She's really had sex, thought Simon. Whoa. A year ago, he would have run back to Kowloon and hidden under his bed. Now he just wanted to think of something to say to her other than "Yeah." He looked over at the school and the court.

"Like a basketball coach who cannot play basketball," he offered. "Kind of. Look at the bird," he said, trying to think of something else to say.

But she was off again. About her school. About the world. About parents. He nodded at first, but then stopped following. After a while, she apologized for all her "crapping on."

"It's good for my English," he joked.

"Cool," she replied.

And they looked out over the sea. But their silence wasn't comfortable, and the day seemed to die out as it continued. She'd said almost everything and he'd said almost nothing.

He closed his eyes. As if he gave a damn about improving his English! The only point of English was so he could talk to her. But he just couldn't talk about stuff the way she could, though he could understand her. It was almost bad how well he could understand her. It was like the way he thought. He just couldn't put it into English. He sat there and watched her look like she was alone.

Just try, he thought. You have to. That's what she speaks.

But monks, telephone books, islands . . . How would he ever put all that together? He knew what she meant but . . . What was she looking for in her bag? A watch? Her iPod? Her ticket?

"I can't say my thought to you. I want to when you speak about . . . many things. Agree. Disagree. Most agree. But I can just follow. Ahh! Sorry. One time I saw this guy on TV. He understands people who say things to him, everything they say, but he can't communicate. Can only move his eye. I always think I will go crazy if I am him. And now I am him."

"Simon . . . you . . ." She looked at him and shook her head. "Can you tell me what happened at school? I mean I know it's bullshit, but it's not all bullshit and I don't know. . ."

There was no way, he thought. He'd never even put it together in Chinese.

"Sorry, forget it," she said.

"I can't pass English," he said. "When I . . . when I study, I just always see no change in my result, just study every day and no change or maybe a little change or maybe going back. Before I met you, I never use anything I study except in exam. Never speak. Nothing. Everything I can't see a reason. Just I must believe in my teacher. So it's not to study for myself with my mind open, just to pray with my blind eyes. Like the praying guy." He watched her smile and lost his train of thought momentarily.

"So I . . . I cannot see my point. Maybe there is no point. So pointless. Yes. Study for many hours and still cannot speak anything. Cannot use my English for anything. Only new words and new grammar. Like telephone books. But I never find the names in exam!"

He laughed and she laughed back.

"So what did you do?"

"The other subjects also were not so good after I spend too much time studying just one subject. So everything was fall behind. So I stop studying English too much and I fall back to my old class minus one and then pass Certificate is impossible . . . so I give up my school . . . that's it." And he nodded.

"Shit," she said. "I could help you with your English and maybe you could help me with my math. What do you think? We'll discuss it when we get back to Hong Kong."

Simon smiled. "Really?" The thought of spending more time with her made him happy though he held out no hope of passing.

"Problem solved," she said, and dug out her drink bottle. They shared the warm water, then picked up their backpacks and headed deep into the island.

24

The dirt lanes behind the main street were dark and cool, too narrow for any light but the highest sun. Wooden planks stretched out between the shops and bridged the ditches. Gangs of tricycle riders sped by like posses in the Wild West. Simon and Amy walked past a store selling outdated clothing, cheap toys, and snacks; a butcher shop; a video store; a dark shop greasy with machine parts; and a doctor's office.

When they emerged from the last lane they screamed and whispered and giggled. It was the coolest and spookiest place ever.

"You'd never think it from looking at the main street," said Amy.

Simon agreed. "Hungry?"

"I am so hungry!"

They followed some locals to a wide dirt street that cut the island in half long-ways and found food carts lined up on the corner. They bought sausages and grilled chicken and sat back-to-back on the curb to eat them. No food ever tasted so good. The chicken was salty and golden and the sausages were crisp and oily. When they were done, they licked their fingers and sighed with pleasure. But the smell of custard waffles brought back their appetite, and they had to try one apiece before moving on.

"Oh jeez," she said, still sitting on the ground. "Which way? I can't move."

"I think there is a beach on the other side."

"Well, it's an island," said Amy.

"You're so smart." He laughed and started to get up.

"Wait," said Amy. "We can help each other. You push into my back and I'll push into yours."

"What?"

"Don't worry, you'll get it." Then she counted to three and pushed, but they didn't rise. "Come on," she said. "Try harder. One. Two . . . oh, wait. Link arms! Okay. One. Two. All right!"

As soon as they were up, Amy leaned forward and pulled Simon onto the rack of her back.

"Uhh. Enough," Simon groaned.

Then she put him down, and he returned the favor.

"Simon!"

"I think I'm winnuh!"

"Dream on."

On the way up the hill, she dug out her earphones and pushed one in his ear. The music almost burst his eardrum.

"Oh shit, sorry," she mumbled, and turned the volume down. He heard muffled English singing and a lot of isolated bass guitar, but he didn't mind.

"Wow," she said once they reached the top. The back bay did have a beach, and the water stretched on forever.

On a concrete promenade, they watched the colors of the island come alive as the sun lost its power. The sea became more blue. The mountains more green. The cottages light red, orange, and lime. Then Amy took off down the stone steps and Simon walked off in search of beer.

"You got it!" she shouted.

"Yeah," he said, like it wasn't one of his proudest accomplishments. There had been a bottle shop behind an empty lifeguard hut. The owner hadn't asked for his ID.

They opened the bottles immediately. It was like drinking cool sunlight. He loved the taste. She told him an old joke she remembered from primary school. He didn't get the punchline: "'I'm afraid not,' said the rope. You get it? I'm . . . a . . . frayed . . . knot!"

He looked at her like she was crazy.

"A frayed knot is a knot that's almost going to fall apart. You know, like rope that's fraying. So a frayed knot equals 'afraid not,' like 'I'm afraid not'! Get it? A frayed knot. It's cool, isn't it?"

"That's San Francisco joke?"

"Yeah, it's a classic! All right, you tell me a Chinese joke."

Simon translated one of his favorites.

"I don't get it," said Amy as Simon trailed off in hysterics. "But I bet it's so funny," then she cracked up too, just from looking at him. "Okay, here's one. It's amazing. This horse walks up to a bar and the bartender says, 'Why the long face?'"

Simon thought about it for a moment. "A bartender is a person?"

"Yeah," said Amy, "he works in the bar. And that's what they say if a customer looks sad. You know, 'Why the long face?'"

"To horses?"

"Well, that's the joke. See? 'Why the long face?' It's funny because the horse always has a long face, so he can't help it."

"Are you sure?"

"Ah, piss off," she said and poked him in the stomach.

He reached out and caught her hand.

"Yes?" she said, gently challenging him.

She almost kissed him then but let the moment pass.

There was too much going on in her life, and she didn't want to make things more complicated.

Simon sensed the moment too, but it went by so quickly, he wasn't sure if he'd imagined it. He did spend a lot of time thinking about kissing her.

It was confusing being friends with the girl of your dreams, but it was definitely okay. Having her lean against him as the sun went down was almost the perfect ending to the best day he'd ever had.

25

Oh god, thought Amy. She recognized the shoes outside the front door. What was he doing there a week early? She snuck into the kitchen to compose herself.

"Amy, come say hello to your father."

"I'm just putting my bag down, Mom."

"Where have you been all day?"

"Studying." On an island.

She grabbed for her hairbrush. She dawdled with her books. She didn't need to empty her bag in the kitchen, but she did. Sand followed.

"Guess what!" Nathan called.

"Yes, I know," said Amy.

"No, you don't."

She walked in. Mr. Lee was sitting on the couch patting Nathan's head, and Mrs. Lee was sitting next to him. Her father looked the same, with his mop of hair and long legs. What was her mother doing holding his hand?

"Dad's going to take us back to San Francisco!" Nathan shouted.

"What?"

"We still need to discuss a few things," her mother said. "But perhaps we will return in May."

"No. No, no, no."

"She likes dumplings too much," her father said. The comment startled Amy even further but she recovered quickly. Only her mother noticed her discomfort. "How is the doctor?"

"They're having a little fight."

"Mom."

"Don't worry, Amy," said Nathan. "Soon we'll be back home!"

"Hold your horses, Nathan," said Mrs. Lee. "This weekend we can talk about it. Everyone together in Sai Kung. Grandma and Grandpa Lee are looking forward to seeing you so much. Both of you," she added, looking at her daughter.

26

The next day Simon wore his white school pants to work. He was feeling optimistic after his day on the island and decided to set his sights on waitering again. A change of clothes and a more positive attitude could bring success.

The cooks laughed, but it didn't bother him. He put on a waiter's apron and went through the words on the specials board, making note of the ones he didn't know until they numbered too many. Over the sink, he practiced holding two coffee cups with their saucers in one hand. No one asked him about his day off.

* * *

Amy was at the Mongkok clinic in a state of panic. She'd canceled Saturday but the clinic couldn't reschedule her until the first week of May. But by that time, she could be on a plane home. The only time she could do it was the weekend after Nathan's birthday. Her father would be away on business again before coming back in early May. It was like he was some white knight all of a sudden. What bullshit, thought Amy. She was furious at how everyone, especially her mother, had forgiven him so easily.

"There must be something!" she said, in English.

"You could try a private clinic," the receptionist said.

"No, I can't. I don't have the money. I already—"

"You can go to the mainland. The mainland is more cheaper."

"What? China?"

"Shenzhen."

"How far is that?"

"Not far. Only one train ride."

"Will it be safe?"

"Yes. If you go to a hospital."

"Really? Can I schedule by phone?"

The lines were scratchy and the receptionists weren't used to speaking English. They didn't get it that Amy was Chinese but didn't speak Chinese. They asked about America. She didn't understand their directions. She freaked out. She sat down in front of some bank or government building and cried. There were too many things to handle. It wasn't going to work out. She tried to hide herself in her music until it got dark. The city air felt suffocating, like a homeless person's quilt. Then it got dark.

But she couldn't go home yet. She had to figure something out. Her Chinese wouldn't be better tomorrow.

Jordan could help her. But she'd have to plead with him to make the calls and she didn't think she could. She'd end up saying what she thought of him or hanging up on him again. Her classmates were out of the question. Jordan's friends were out of the question. The only person she knew who she could trust was the one she really didn't want to tell.

Simon's white-pants day was going quite well. At lunch he'd been allowed to clear plates. It led him to daydreams of getting paid as a waiter and taking Amy to a seafood restaurant when she finished her exams.

By the end of dinner, he was back doing drinks, but studying the waiters whenever he could. Then he got his second-ever phone call at work.

"Simon!" Olga shouted. "Quickly!"

"Drinks and ashtrays next," said Nigel.

Simon nodded and picked up.

"Katie," he said.

"Who's Katie?" said Amy.

Oh, shit.

"Sorry, I know you're busy. You're really busy, I can hear. I'll call you another time."

"No. It's okay. I'm fine," he said.

"Yeah? Okay, well, I have kind of this problem and . . . I was wondering if you could help me." He heard her voice break. It surprised both of them.

"Of course."

"I just . . . I've been trying . . ." She let out a nervous laugh. "What have I been trying? . . . Now I don't know what to say. Um . . . can you meet me somewhere?"

"When? Now?" he said.

"No. When you finish. Is that like an hour or so? I'm sorry about this."

"Are you okay?"

"Yeah." Her voice did that thing again. "It's . . ." She let out a strained laugh, not like her. "I'll explain later."

"Where are you?"

"In Central Station."

"Where?"

"Near the ferry exits."

"Okay. I'll be there."

"Whenever. Don't rush, okay? I'll be fine."

"Drinks!"

Simon replaced the phone, then looked over to Olga and Nigel.

"Useless," said Olga.

Nigel gave him an exaggerated look of disappointment. "Come on. Get your tray."

Simon stood where he was for a moment, then started taking off his apron.

"Not in here," said Olga. Simon didn't seem to hear her. Pierre the chef was at the bar too, holding a beer. "Look, he doesn't understand," said Olga.

The chef nodded and snarled. Nigel commented on Simon's now-exposed white pants. Everyone laughed. Simon felt the heat rise to his face.

"Excuse me," he said, and moved past Nigel.

"What now?" said Olga, shaking her head.

"Simon," Nigel sung out, gesturing to a table of empties and ashtrays. "Hurry up."

"Tray!" said Olga.

"I'm not your dog," said Simon, almost shaking. It was the first time he had ever raised his voice to an adult.

"Is he talking to me?" asked Olga.

"I'm sorry. I have to leave. Good-bye," said Simon.

"Is he talking to me?"

Nigel raised his eyebrows and whistled.

Halfway down the street, Simon still felt like someone was going to grab him from behind, but he wouldn't run until he was out of sight. His heart was beating so hard that he could feel his pulse in his fingers. Toward the bottom he realized he'd left behind his schoolbag and day's pay. Keep them, he thought, and took off toward the subway.

27

Simon bounded down the flat escalator, scanning everything as he passed. He wasn't worried about not finding her. Spotting her in a crowded station was his specialty. He just wondered what she'd look like when he found her.

She was at a bookstand, flicking through a magazine.

"Amy!"

She jumped. "Wow. Did you just run here?"

He shrugged. "Yeah."

"You didn't have to," she told him, but it made her smile. She gave him a quick hug. Then her face got serious again. They walked over to a space in the corner of the hall. There was no good way to say it.

"I can't believe I'm telling you this . . . but, um . . ."

"It's okay," he replied, now almost as nervous as she was. What was it that she so clearly didn't want him to know? He couldn't think of anything that could change the way he thought about her.

"I need to get an abortion."

"Hmm?"

He wondered if she was in danger somehow. It sounded like some kind of visa or operation. He'd heard the word, but he couldn't remember it exactly. He gave his lack-of-comprehension look, which made him appear to be frowning.

Amy winced.

"I don't know what it is," he told her. "I don't know what is that."

"It's when . . . it's when you're pregnant and you have to . . . you want to . . ."

"Oh. I know."

Her eyes filled as she watched his cloud over. But he was just checking to see if he felt as bad as she seemed to think he should. But he didn't. It was still Amy in front of him, and he felt exactly the way he always had.

"Okay," he said. "What can we do?"

"Well, um . . . ," she began, still watching him like a hawk. "I made an appointment but now my dad's here so I tried to reschedule, but there's no space at this clinic so . . ."

"Uh-huh," he said, trying to sound positive.

"So I'm trying to get one in . . . Shenzhen."

"For tomorrow?"

"No, not that soon. The week after next."

"Oh."

"But I can't make an appointment on the phone. I've been trying. But my Chinese . . . I need someone who can . . ."

"Speak Chinese? Easy," he said.

"Easy, huh?"

"Yes."

"You do this all the time?"

"Yes. All the time!"

She punched him in the shoulder, her laughter not far from tears. Then she looked serious again and Simon could tell there was something else.

"I can't be with you when you call because I've got this 'family meeting' thing this weekend at my grandparents'. Dad shows up two days ago and it's like everything's worked out between him and my mom. So they're thinking of taking us back to San Francisco and we're going up to Sai Kung to discuss it or something."

"I can do it," he said, as he felt his world collapse.

"Nothing's set, of course . . . about going back to San

Francisco. I'm pretty sure they'll change their minds. They always do. But anyway . . . that's where I'll be tomorrow and the weekend."

"Okay," he said, trying to smile.

"So who's Katie, hey?"

"She's a friend from my school."

"I see," she said, cocking an eyebrow, acting like it wouldn't hurt her.

28

She grunted "library" on her way out and slammed the door. A whole weekend of playing the good daughter was too much when you had grown-up problems. She tried to distract herself with fashion as she walked the busy streets. She noticed a pair of knee-high boots, lavender eye shadow, a tan business suit.

The last few days she had started to feel a little different. She didn't think she was imagining things. It was sort of like a period, though the feeling was mostly on top. She wasn't showing yet, but being pregnant made her think of the weight she'd put on since she'd come to Hong Kong. She wasn't a beanpole anymore like her father. She was turning into the other one. These days she looked like a photo she kept of her mother just before she got married.

She walked into the lobby and saw Simon get out of an elevator. The hotel she'd recommended was more of a palace than a skyscraper. Everything inside was shining.

"Were you checking out the rooms?" she said.

"No," he replied, flustered. He'd been up to look at the restaurant.

"Just looking around? So what do you think?"

"It's beautiful place."

He tried to smile, but she could tell he was uncomfortable.

"Let's get out of here," she said without a second thought.

They stopped at a sliver of a sushi bar. It was so narrow they could have held hands and touched the walls on each side. The counter was the width of a stair. Amy loved it. They picked individually wrapped pieces of cheap sushi out of a refrigerator. He hardly ever ate sushi but he didn't mind.

They didn't want to say the things they had to say. They wanted everything to stay as it was. It was Easter break and they wanted to be like the other teens walking around.

"It looks like my mom and dad are together again. And they want to take us home next month."

Simon took a deep breath and nodded. He'd made himself expect the worst, but it still felt like he'd eaten too much wasabi.

"I can't believe my mom's taking him back. He cheated on her, you know. Maybe she'll still change her mind."

"I hope," he said, and cleared his throat. Then he pulled some notepaper out of his pocket. "I have a list from the hospital."

"Oh. Cool. Wow. Thank you."

"I didn't write the time of the train but I will write later."

"You don't have to do that."

"I already but I forgot to bring."

"You mean you don't carry it around with you? God, I can't rely on anyone."

Simon looked at her for a moment, not sure she was kidding.

"Simon! I'm not serious." She laughed, but her face broke suddenly and she looked on the edge of tears.

"God."

"Don't worry," he said.

"I'm always like this nowadays. Everything. It's pathetic."

"No. It's okay. Everything is okay."

"So do you think this place is a good one? In China?"

"Yes, I think okay. I'll take you there."

"You'll what? You don't have to do that."

He shrugged.

"What about your job? You can't lose your job."

"I'm looking for a new job."

"What?! When did that happen?"

"It's long story."

"Simon," she half giggled, half scolded.

"The hospital is maybe less than one hour from Kowloon by KCR train. I will organize transport."

"You seriously want to go with me?"

"Of course."

Her eyes teared up. "That'd be really good. But how can I help you? I need to do something for you."

"I'm okay."

"Can't I help with your Certificate exam? The English one."

Simon flinched.

"We could study every day. It's not for another two weeks or so, right?"

He nodded.

"I could just say I was sick or . . . I don't care. My exams aren't till next year . . . if I'm here then."

He shook his head.

"But none of the people I know are as good as you. I mean, I can't talk to any of them like I can talk to you. And your emails . . ."

"The exam is different."

"Yeah, but . . . Yeah, you're right."

He gathered together their plastic wrappings and containers. She knew she should drop it but it wasn't in her nature.

"Can't we just try? I mean, maybe I could help. It is my stupid language."

His stomach churned.

She followed him out to the noisy street. She had to shout.

"You can even tell jokes in English, though they're not as good as mine. I can't believe how much you've improved since I met you and you haven't even been studying!"

He laughed at that. He'd been studying a lot, more than he had in class, just not textbooks.

"I don't see how you and I could fuck it up," she said, then burst out laughing.

Simon smiled but his insides were on fire. It was one thing to disappoint himself. What if she realized he was just dumb?

"Okay," he said.

29

They met in the food court of Festival Walk mall. Simon gave her a lot of loose English papers he'd stuffed in a binder and pushed under his bed, three textbooks, and a dictionary.

"Wow, there's so much," she said after a while. "Do you want to start with this one? What are the prepositions that go with the verbs?

"It belongs blank you," she began.

"For you," said Simon.

"*To* you," she corrected. "How about this one: We're going blank holiday to Thailand."

"To holiday," Simon said confidently.

"Makes sense. It's not what they have in the book, but it makes sense. The book had *on* holiday." She looked for another exercise.

"How about . . . The building was next to a shop *was selling* delicious snacks, or *selling* delicious snacks?"

"*Was selling* delicious snacks."

"Are you sure?"

"The other one."

"Right! . . . next to a shop *selling* delicious snacks. Because you don't say, . . . next to a shop *was selling* delicious snacks. You say *selling* delicious snacks . . . because . . . I don't know. Is there an explanation key somewhere?"

He shook his head. "I don't think."

"I don't think *so*," she mumbled. "Don't worry, I'll look it up in the grammar book. Just a sec."

Half an hour later, Amy was lost in a chapter about adjectival clauses, relative pronouns, complete verbs, present and past participles, reduced adjective clauses. Holy shit, she thought to herself.

"It's pretty complicated, isn't it?" she said. "Wow. Cool. Sorry, I just want to make sure I know what I'm . . . Let me just finish this one . . . thing and . . ." She drifted off again.

Simon smiled as he made his way over to the food stalls. He didn't feel unlucky to be at the only table covered in schoolbooks.

* * *

155

Okay, thought Amy, so *present simple* is I eat, you eat, she eats. *Present continuous* is I am eating, you are eating, etc. *Present perfect* is have or has plus past participle. I have eaten. She has eaten. *Present perfect continuous* is . . .

"Present perfect continuous?! You know what that is?"

Simon nodded.

"Seriously," said Amy. "Very good."

Simon looked at an old vocabulary list and considered which words he still knew: *introduction, example, vitamins, manufacture, dosage, dose, standard (manufacturing standards), objective, subjective, report, regulation, to regulate, hostages, terrorist, to give up hope, inhabitants, overweight, privacy, shrink, obligation, duty, queue, seminar, function, to hold a seminar/function, waterskiing, surfing, ancestors, descendants, candidate, election.* La la la la la.

Amy was smiling at something. It made Simon smile too before he saw what she was looking at. One of his old exam papers had been left inside his textbook. He thought he'd thrown them all out.

"It's so cute. You said, 'The driver was so afraid and had many water on his face.' Do you know what we call that?"

Simon thought about it for a moment. He knew it in Chinese.

"Sweat," said Amy. "S-w-e-a-t."

"Also, you have, 'I saw a policeman *fell down*.' It should be I saw a policeman *fall* down. And I'm not sure why. Sorry."

She'd tried to figure it out without looking in a grammar book, but the story happened in the past, so why not write it that way? She thought she was the worst teacher ever.

He wondered how many more ridiculous things he'd written.

By the end of the first week, Amy had decided to go to China by herself. It was already bad enough that she couldn't help him with the one thing he needed. There was no way she was dragging him to China, too. What he must think of her already made her cringe. But she was determined to give his Certificate one last do-or-die effort before she freed him completely. English could not be so complicated. Maybe if she saw more of the practice exams, she thought, it would turn things around. So far, she'd seen only one. Somehow the others had all been lost.

"What about Kelly?"

"Who?"

"You know. The girl you were talking to . . . you know."

Simon looked back at his papers.

"Come on. You said her name the other day. On the phone. Kay . . . Kylie . . . Kayla?"

"Katie."

"Yeah. What about her? Maybe she has some old exams. Is she any good at English?"

Simon nodded.

"Cool. She could explain a few things to me, then. And maybe give us two or three old exams."

Simon shrugged.

"I'm being nosy again, aren't I? You don't want me to. That's okay. I'm sorry." She looked down at all the notes.

"No, no. It's fine. Yeah, good idea."

"Awesome. Let's do it, then. We can ask her today so we can start tomorrow."

Great, thought Simon, wondering how he was going to put it to Katie. She would think he was insane for waiting this long to start studying again. *Why didn't you let me help you?* he could hear her ask. He'd have to fix it so the two of them never actually spoke to each other. He would say the exams were for a non-Chinese-speaking friend. Also non-English speaking.

"Who?" said Katie. "What friend?"

"You know, um, that guy . . . I play . . ."

"Simon, I know it's for you. Are you studying?"

"Maybe," he looked over at Amy. She was close enough to hear the conversation but it was in Chinese.

"Simon. Why didn't you start earlier? I think it's too late now!"

"No, don't worry. I'm just doing it for experience. I have some spare time at the moment, so I thought why not."

"What about the other subjects? Do you need . . . have

you asked someone else about them?"

"No, I think they're okay."

"So you're not working at the restaurant now?"

"Not now. I'm applying for a job at this other place. It's fine." He smiled at Amy.

"Have you got something good to wear for the party?"

"Huh?" said Simon.

"Next Friday. So near!"

He'd forgotten about the graduation party.

"When do you want to pick up the exams? You know you can buy them at a bookstore." She laughed.

"Really?"

"It's okay. You can take some of mine. I've finished."

"Thanks."

"You have to study every day at least ten hours. You know?"

"What? Only ten?" said Simon. "Maybe I can get a better result if you don't study so hard and push my result lower."

"Crazy guy."

Amy was trying to get his attention. He put his hand over the mouthpiece. "What?" he asked Amy in Chinese. "I mean, what?" he said in English.

"I was thinking . . ." Amy began.

Simon felt the phone begin to vibrate with Katie's voice. "Are you speaking English?"

"I was thinking maybe we could all study together one time," Amy continued. "Katie could explain things to you and I could maybe ask her some things and—"

"Who's talking to you in English?"

"Um . . ."

"Hi, Katie," Amy called out.

"Who just said my name? Simon, what's going on?"

"It's just . . . a girl I met . . ."

"What girl?"

"I met her on my train and she's helping me with some English. That's all."

"What girl on the train?"

"It doesn't matter."

"Is she your girlfriend?"

"No."

"What school does she go to?"

"I don't know. Somewhere in Yau Ma Tei."

"Oh my god. She's the one the boys always talk about, isn't she? I knew it. Steven and Raymond said . . ."

"No."

"Does she want to speak with me?"

"No."

"Can I?" asked Amy, stepping beside him and putting her hand out for the phone. She was smiling. He handed over the receiver. Katie was still speaking in Chinese when Amy came on.

"Hello. Katie?"

"Yes, I'm Katie."

"Hi, I'm Amy."

"Yes. What do you want?"

"Maybe Simon told you that I'm trying to help him with his English but I'm hopeless at it, and I just thought that if I knew a little more about what was on the exam . . . Maybe I could ask you a few questions sometime?"

"You want to help him pass the exam?"

"Yeah, I know. Is that crazy? I speak English, but I realize you have to know a lot about the exam, too, and he always says you're the best student."

"I'm just okay."

"Well, better than me."

"You are American?" Katie asked.

"Yes. And Chinese. Sort of."

"I see," said Katie in her formal English. "So you would like for me to tell you about the Hong Kong Certificate of English exam."

"Yes, that'd be great."

"When?"

"Whenever you can?"

"Come to my house tomorrow morning at nine thirty," said Katie. "Then we can talk."

She gave her address.

"Fantastic," said Amy. "Do you want to speak to Simon?"

"No."

30

"You are very pretty," Katie said in English.

"No," said Amy.

"I can't believe you don't speak Chinese," Katie said, in Chinese.

"Sorry?"

"Never mind. Hi, I'm Katie."

"Hi, I'm Amy. Thanks for coming down to get me."

Amy noticed Katie was on the heavy side but cute all the same. She smiled.

"Simon is my best friend," said Katie. "How long have you known him?"

"Not long."

Katie looked Amy over once more, then shot off up the old concrete stairs. "I know why all the boys want to be your friend," she called from above.

"Sorry?"

"Two more floors."

Katie's apartment block was from old Hong Kong. The concrete was weather stained and the paint was chipped and faded. Katie pushed open the fifth door of the fourth balcony. The walls smelled of years of Chinese cooking and old furniture. The living room was the size of Amy's bedroom. The kitchen was the size of her family's bathroom. Katie's was the only bedroom. Amy sat on a bottom bunk and wondered where the parents slept. Katie went to the kitchen and brought back two iced teas. She took a sip, then stared at Amy.

"You want to help Simon pass his Certificate exam?"

"Yeah, but it's more difficult than I thought."

"I also tried to help him pass. But he is too . . ." Katie searched for the word, then said "pig-headed" in Chinese. "Do you understand?"

"Proud?"

"No. Like a pig. Stubborn. I offer to help with my tutor but he only wants to study his way and then he stops to study."

"Oh . . . At least now he's trying again."

"Of course, I will help if he asks me. I don't care. But it

163

makes me feel upset. I think he waste his . . . chance." Katie sighed. "Does he study now?"

"Yeah."

"Unbelievable. He likes you so much."

"Why do you say that?"

Katie shook her head. "Nobody can make him speak English. Secondly, he doesn't notice any girls."

"He's never had a girlfriend?"

"No!"

Amy laughed. "Why not?"

Katie shrugged. "I don't know. Some girls like him. But he never shows interest."

"Which girls?"

"Just girls at school."

"Did they ever tell him?"

"I don't know. Maybe. He wouldn't notice anyway. I used to like him."

"Yeah? What happened?"

"Nothing. But it was a long time ago. He's not my type now."

Amy smiled. "Who's your type now?"

Katie pointed at her posters of Cristiano Ronaldo. "I like Latin guys.

"So you want to be Simon's girlfriend?"

Amy let out a nervous laugh. "No. We're friends. Good

friends. And I want to help him with his . . . uh . . ."

"Are you sure you don't want him to be your boyfriend?"

"I don't have much luck with boys, to tell the truth, and, well . . . I don't think I'm going to be here much longer. I think I have to go back to America."

"Does Simon know?"

"Yeah. We don't really talk about it, though."

"He's going to be sad."

"Maybe not that sad. I'm not a lot of fun these days."

Katie didn't look convinced. "He doesn't have so many friends. I think he doesn't speak to anyone from school now. He never even told me about you even though you are famous."

"Famous? What do you mean?"

Katie paused. "You are called Subway Girl."

"Subway Girl? I kind of like it."

"I think everyone would be jealous, but he doesn't say. Even to me. Maybe they will think he and you are . . . you know . . ."

"What?"

Katie blushed. "I know you are not that kind but . . . some boys think you are slutty girl."

"Did Simon say that?"

"No. Simon doesn't say anything. I told you."

Amy exhaled a little nervously.

"I bet he wants to go with you instead of me to the graduation dance."

"What? To where?"

"Our end-of-year party. He didn't say to you?"

"No," said Amy.

"Stupid boy."

Amy tried not to be upset, but she couldn't help it. She'd told herself he would see her differently once he knew about everything. But she hadn't believed it until then.

31

Simon did the first of Katie's practice exams on Sunday, and the grammar section was as unknowable as ever. A second one turned out the same. It worried him because of Amy. He was sure she'd lose faith in him like his teachers had. She'd stopped talking except to correct things. He wanted to get rid of the books and the tests and the notes but he didn't know how. On Tuesday he took her to a sports bar on the harbor, but she corrected his exams while the boats passed.

On Wednesday it was raining and the walk to the mall from the subway station was dark and slick. He planned to take her to a funny movie if he could or a horror movie if she preferred. It was only three days till the operation, and she'd be in need of cheering up. He was nervous about China too. They spoke Cantonese Chinese over the phone in the Shenzhen hospitals, but he wondered if the stationmasters did as well or if they spoke in Mandarin Chinese like the rest of the mainland. What if he misunderstood a train announcement and didn't get her there on time? He planned to leave early just in case.

He'd bought a tiny alarm clock and tested it that morning. He planned to pack some food in case she was hungry afterward and didn't like the food over there. He had his ID card. He'd wait until the day before to remind Amy about hers. She wouldn't want him reminding her about anything now. He wondered if they'd be coming back in the dark. He'd bring a warm jacket for her too. And a hat.

She was at the usual table. He noticed she wasn't wearing her school uniform for the second day in a row. It confirmed to him that she was leaving Hong Kong.

He skidded up to their table. She didn't look up. He drummed his fingers on the table and smiled.

"Okay. Today, one hundred percent. I can feel it."

"Sorry," she said. "Same again." She showed him the exam she'd been correcting. "I mean, I don't know a lot of these either. Like I don't know why it's wrong to say *learn* knowledge instead of *gain* knowledge. Can't you learn knowledge? I don't think it matters. I really don't, but . . ." She trailed off.

"I can remember for next time."

She nodded but couldn't say anything. It was the worst silence.

"You know that movie . . ."

"About Friday night . . . ," she began at the same time.

They each gave a nervous laugh, then Amy continued.

"Your graduation party is this Friday night, right?"

"What?" He hadn't wanted her to know.

"Don't worry. It's cool. Katie told me."

"I want to tell you but . . ."

"Why? No. It's your party. It's the last time you'll see most of your friends, isn't it?"

He didn't know.

"I wish I'd gone to mine. I kind of left before I had the chance. It'll be great. I'm jealous."

He shook his head. "I want to tell you but the next day . . . you are . . ."

"No, I understand. And it's a nightmare for you to have to think about . . . *that* at your party. And then to get up at dawn."

"It's okay. I have an alarm clock. And maybe I won't stay late. I think a little boring. Just speech and . . ."

"And waiting for me while I have an operation won't be boring?"

He shrugged. "I can see Shenzhen."

"Come on. I've heard about Shenzhen."

"What?" He tried to smile.

"It's so cool of you to offer. But it's fine. I've taken enough trains in my life. It can't be that difficult. I've got the address. I can just show it to a taxi driver, right?"

"But . . ."

"You've done too much already. I wish I'd never . . . I never had to tell you about this. I feel stupid and . . . anyway, I wish I could've helped you more with your English and—"

"Amy . . ."

"Here," she said, and took out her iPod. "I want you to have this."

"No. What are you doing? You need it."

"Will you take it, please?" she insisted.

"Give it to me later."

Then he felt her hands putting the phones to his ears and everything was bad. His body was turning to stone. Then the earphones came to life.

"Shit!" she said, quickly turning down the volume. "God, sorry. I did it again."

"Doesn't matter."

"This is the one you were playing," she mumbled. "See if you can get the words."

"Okay," he heard himself reply.

She put the leather cover in his bag.

No, he thought. But he didn't stop her.

"I want to know how everything goes. Okay?"

Then she rose.

"So anyway . . . I'm shit with good-byes. I think it's better to say it now, though. When I get back, I'll probably just be a zombie for a little while or I don't know, and we'll be packing stuff. I'm sorry I didn't tell you earlier. I didn't want to distract you any more than I already have."

It was too fast. He wasn't ready.

"I'll email you," she said.

He needed words to keep them together, but he wasn't finding them. He half stood up. He wasn't sure what to do.

They gave each other a hug.

"I'm gonna cry," she said and grabbed her things. "I'm sorry."

"Why?" he asked.

"Everything."

He didn't understand.

"I have to go," she said.

"Okay," he said and looked down at his pile of books as she walked away. Then he shot a look across the floor and found her black hair and blue coat and wondered if he was watching her disappear into a crowd for the last time.

32

The graduation party was at The Grand Palm resort and conference center in Causeway Bay. Katie had asked to meet at the entrance instead of in the lobby. That way she wouldn't have to walk in alone. Simon was wearing a light blue nylon jacket, his orange shirt, jeans, and new sneakers. It had been two days since Amy had left, and he'd thought about her every minute since. He'd written her once, but could hardly get anything down except a stupid question about Chinese food in America. She hadn't emailed back. He zipped his jacket. It was windy.

Katie stepped out of a taxi. He'd never seen her look so grown-up.

"You look good," he said.

She had on a high-collared silk cheongsam with an orchid pin.

She frowned. "Really?"

"I'm serious. How about me?"

"Yeah, you're fine. Are a lot of people here already?" she asked, her eyes darting around.

"I'm not sure."

The lobby was more modern-looking than the place where he'd met Amy. There was a lot of carpet and not much marble. Katie looked at what the other girls were wearing, then screamed as the most popular students walked in. She ran over and linked arms with the only other person in her English class who wasn't attached.

Simon thought of going over to say hi to Max but saw him talking happily with two girls. Then he spotted Kenny and Leon, but they were in the middle of a crowd, so he checked out the pool area.

When he made it back to the ballroom, the place was almost full. He saw Katie with her classmates at a table in the front. She gave Simon her two-hand wave and a look of helplessness because she couldn't save him a seat. "It's okay," he called out, then noticed his class table was full too.

The only free seat he saw was with some of the super-achievers of Form 5. They were discussing which teachers they liked and which ones they didn't want for Form 6. Simon figured it could have been worse. He could have been sitting closer to the table in the back, where Steven called out "Hey, waiter," just before he sat down.

The first part of the program was speeches, followed by every class's impression of their homeroom teacher. Then, tables were called out to go to the buffet, and Simon's came first.

"Number one," announced the MC, but not being a class Number One student himself, Simon didn't get up. Too late, he realized it was just a way of identifying his table. He felt a little stupid as he finally stood, and started to wonder what he was doing at the party at all. He glanced around the room, searching for a pal, but ended up back at the entrance. And then he saw her standing just inside the door, looking a little lost herself.

It wasn't a normal surprise because when the thing happens that mirrors exactly what your heart wants, it's more like a dream than a surprise.

"She's here," he whispered.

She hadn't known how he would react. She hoped he'd be happy, but she'd prepared herself to turn around and leave if he'd looked upset or even angry. He walked straight over and took her hand with a smile that lit up the room for her.

"Hi."

"Hi."

"I thought you might want to speak English to some-one," she said.

"Yeah, of course. Always."

"Good. Well, here I am."

"How did you . . . ?" he began. "I thought . . ."

"Yeah, sorry." Her face fell. She didn't want to tell him how crazy she'd been feeling.

"Are you thirsty?" he asked.

"A little. Oh . . . ," she said as she saw what the other girls were wearing. "I thought this was a disco party." She buttoned up her coat. Simon didn't know what she was talking about.

"It's okay," he said.

"You always say that."

"Please come to my table."

"Sure."

She sat in Simon's chair as he went to look for another, and smiled at the people coming back from the buffet. She thought some of the girls in the room were beautiful. She noticed one girl in a sexy blouse and it made her feel more at ease. A couple of guys began to turn her way, including a couple she sort of recognized.

"I'm sorry," Simon said a few minutes later. "My teach-ers wanted to talk with me."

"Really?"

"No."

She rolled her eyes.

"Can I get you something?"

"I don't think I can eat. Can I?"

"Oh, yeah." He kicked himself.

"It's okay," she said. Part of her liked that he'd forgotten. "But a water would be good."

"We can go. Anytime you want," he told her.

"But I just got here."

She told him to eat for her. He brought back two waters and spilled one of them immediately.

"Oh shit," he said.

"Nice waiter," she said.

They started to giggle, and each time one of them would try to stop, the other would begin afresh until they had to stop looking at each other.

The room went quiet when the presentations began, and Simon thought how it was lucky after all that Katie had sat with her classmates instead of with him. He and Amy could just hang out. But when Katie stopped by and didn't look surprised to see Amy, Simon realized it was his old friend who'd gotten Amy to come. She hadn't abandoned him at all. It made him almost as happy as when he'd seen Amy at the door.

"So, how much did you study today?" Katie asked in

Chinese. "Remember, only five more days."

"Of course ten hours," said Simon. "I'm nearly blind."

"Good."

Amy hugged Katie as the lights dimmed for a final speech.

"It's Subway Girl. I know it," mumbled Eric, watching from the guys' table in the back. "She looks different but I know it's her."

"Everybody!" said Raymond. "Eric says Subway Girl has come to visit us tonight."

The guys at the table laughed.

"As if," said Steven, only half paying attention. "Which?"

The girl Eric pointed to had no purple streaks, no school uniform, and no legendary earphones.

"It's not her, you idiot," said Steven.

The music went up as the lights went down and the teachers began to leave. Small lanterns were lit on the tables and the stage became a dance floor. Amy loved it. Simon was apprehensive, though he tried not to show it.

Amy went outside to help Katie get a cab. Simon heard his Chinese name being called by the guys at the back. He turned around when Amy had left the room.

"Finally," said Steven.

"What do you want?" asked Simon.

"Two beers, please. And make it fast."

Everyone laughed.

"Would you like a brain with that?" replied Simon. Speaking was so easy in Chinese.

Eric giggled. Steven imitated his giggle. "So who's the girl you were sitting next to?" Everyone went quiet.

"A friend," said Simon.

"It's Subway Girl," said Eric. "I'm telling you."

"I want to meet her," said Steven.

"It's a free country," said Simon.

"You already have," said Eric. "It's her!"

"Bullshit. What's her name?"

"Amy," said Simon. "All right. I'm going. Nice to see you again," he added in English.

"I told you!" said Eric.

"How do you know her name's Amy?"

Then, back to Simon, "No, stay!" he ordered, but Simon had wandered off.

"I saw it on that chat address. Remember?"

"Ah, yeah," said Steven.

"Whoa," said Raymond.

"I told you!" said Eric.

"She's a weirdo," said Steven, like he couldn't care less. But the other guys turned their chairs around to get a better view.

When Amy returned from the lobby, the guys started shouting at her directly. Simon wasn't sure if she understood the calls of "Subway Girl" or heard them say her name, but if she did, she was doing the best job of ignoring them, as usual.

Then she did something quite terrifying.

"Come on," she said and led him up to the stage.

It was like being thrown into the ocean with Aquaman, but at least he was Aquaman's friend.

A few girls, a couple of boyfriends, and a handful of the top students, just out of habit, were the only ones up there. Everyone else milled around the edges. The guys from the back came up and started to point and laugh from the sides. Simon wasn't sure what to do. But Amy kept smiling at him and ignoring the guys until they went away. Finally, when he realized no one was going to attack her like last time with Jordan, he started smiling too. He even placed her hand above her head like another couple was doing, and to his amazement, watched her do a perfect twirl.

"I don't think I can dance anymore," Amy said, almost an hour later. "You've worn me out."

Simon laughed and shook his head. "I'll take you home," he said and held her hand as they walked down the stairs.

She went off to the ladies' room, and he took a last, long look at the ballroom and his classmates, and despite all the crap of school, he felt a wave of sadness, and then he was fine.

They rode the subway to her station. She felt small to him as she snuggled close. He wondered if she would argue with him when he told her he was going to take her to China, but she just nodded. Then they hugged tightly and he could feel her worry. He chanted "Set alarm for five" the rest of his way home.

33

It was still dark when he threw on his clothes, picked up his backpack, and headed out. He was too tired to think of anything except not taking the train past her station and not pressing her apartment buzzer if she wasn't there yet.

She was dressed for the mountains. Hiking with Jordan was her excuse. They mumbled "Hi" and she squeezed his hand before walking on alone. The street lamps were still on.

Halfway to the station she scrunched up her face and put her hand to her stomach.

"Are you okay?"

"Yeah," she said, then walked behind a bench and vomited

even though there was nothing to vomit. He walked closer to her the rest of the way to the station.

They got on the KCR just after six a.m. The ride was quiet. The sun began to come out. It didn't comfort her. It meant she was getting closer. He gave her the iPod she'd given him but she couldn't listen.

Simon thought about taking out the map to check the route even though he'd already checked everything three times. He almost offered her a chocolate bar twice. He wondered what she was thinking. He wondered how dangerous the operation was going to be and if her vomiting had meant anything bad. He tried to seem calm.

She looked at him when everyone started to stand. He nodded and let her get out first.

They stopped on the platform to take out their ID cards. Amy had brought her passport, too. He asked if he could see her picture. She rolled her eyes. The shot had been taken for a trip to Asia when she was little. She had pigtails.

"Who is this?" he asked.

"I wonder."

They crossed an indoor bridge. They were in China.

They walked fast. The sky was the color of concrete, hardly different from the streets and buildings. The city seemed to go on forever, unbroken by sea or mountains. Simon finally found the right bus stop. When the locals didn't speak Cantonese Chinese, Simon knew enough Mandarin to understand directions.

The hospital looked and smelled like other hospitals. They sat on familiar plastic seats. All the magazines were in Chinese. It makes sense, she thought.

Quickly, her name was called.

The doctor was a tall woman. Amy grabbed her bag.

"I'll be back," she said. "I don't think this is it."

"Okay, I'll wait here," he said a little too loudly, then glanced around at the other people. They were looking at the English speakers. He shifted in his seat.

After fifteen minutes, Simon figured that Amy was probably being operated on, and for a moment he stopped breathing. Everything will be okay, he told himself. He just needed to ask someone about the operation again, how long it took, how safe it was. Then she came out again.

"That was just to make sure I'm okay for the procedure."

"Yeah, of course," said Simon.

"The doctor thinks I should be finished by three. Sorry, it's a long time to wait."

"Three o'clock. Okay." He nodded. It was nine thirty.

"I'll be under a general anesthetic so I guess it takes a while to wake up."

"Yes."

She was more talkative, he noticed. It was a good sign. He tried to think of something to continue the conversation.

Then he gave up and tried to be silently reassuring. He wondered if his expression looked optimistic enough. Then they called her.

A nurse told her to change into a hospital gown. It didn't feel good to walk out into the passageway with almost nothing between her and everything else. She tried to swing her legs onto the gurney without embarrassing herself.

The operating room looked like the ones on the hospital shows except no one was wearing a colorful bandana. There were three people there. Only the nurse was a woman. The doctor smiled at her and told her not to worry about anything. It made her feel okay. And then she was counting to twenty. . . .

Simon wandered around the streets of Shenzhen. The city seemed quite new to him, like it was just put together. There was a lot of concrete but it was clean concrete. There were many huge buildings. There was a central walkway with benches and a large fountain. He wondered where all the people were.

Then he detoured off the main streets and saw all the older, smaller shops. It made him think of his lane in Tai Wo Hau—the dingy canned-food store, the dusty windows—and how he didn't want to spend the rest of his life there.

* * *

At two o'clock, the waiting area was full. Simon went straight to the reception desk.

"Amy Lee?"

"One moment."

He stood still and straight. It seemed to take forever for the orderly to return. When he did, the man was frowning. Simon's heart stopped.

"And who are you?"

"Her friend. I'm taking her back."

"She is still asleep."

The orderly said it like it was something Simon would have to put up with. Simon threw his head back and sighed with relief.

"So, she is sleeping now?"

"I just told you."

"Yes!"

He saw her as soon as she turned into the main corridor. She looked pale and sleepy. His heart began to beat madly.

When he reached her, she was thanking the nurse for holding her bag.

"I have," he said.

She walked beside him a little unsteadily. She asked what the time was. She didn't want to go home. She wanted to lie down for a while. He thought of a hostel he had seen on his walk. She couldn't walk that far. He caught his first taxi ever.

The room was tiny. Two singles and a window. Amy lay down and pulled a thin, gray blanket over her clothes. Simon put the other blanket over her too. She used her backpack as a pillow until he found a real one in the closet. He used his spare T-shirt as a pillowcase.

"Genius," he mumbled to himself, then sat on the edge of the other bed and watched over her.

She reached for his hand and held it as she fell asleep.

34

Amy woke up at seven and was frantic. It was dark.

"We have to go," she said as she rose to her feet.

Simon grabbed their bags and led them out. A street market had appeared between the hostel and the main road. Toys and cheap CDs, sunglasses, key chains, spanner sets, vibrators, face readers, and old CD players in plastic wrap caught other people's attention. The two of them got stuck behind a group of Europeans. It was like waiting behind a truck. They couldn't see how much more of the market there was to go. Amy gave up trying.

"Forget it," she mumbled. "I want to go back."

"To Hong Kong?"

"No. The . . . um . . ." Her mind was still cloudy. "The hostel." She pointed back. "I'll call Mom."

Jordan's friends were going to stay at a hostel in the mountains. They'd miscalculated how long the long trail was. It was really long. Everyone was fine, though.

"Where are you now? In the mountains?" her mother asked.

"Yeah, it's really nice. We had dinner at this place next to the beach and walked up this little mountain and watched the sunset on the other side. Everything turned orange and purple. It was so beautiful."

Simon hoped she would stop talking.

"One second," said Amy. Her mother had asked her to put Jordan on the phone. She turned to Simon. "Do you want to be Jordan?"

"What?"

Amy returned to the phone. "He's outside."

"Call me first thing in the morning," said Mrs. Lee.

Finally, Amy replaced the receiver.

"She thinks you are with Jordan?"

"She trusts him," said Amy.

Simon didn't reply.

"I know. It makes me sick, too. Anyway, whatever. You going to call your parents?"

He called. They went back upstairs. The last thing she remembered was a maple leaf on a backpack. Creaky wood. The bed was still warm.

* * *

"Simon?"

"Yeah."

"Are you sleeping?"

"No."

It was the middle of the night. He was staring at the shadows on the walls. She asked him to lie next to her. He got up and she lifted up her blanket. Except for their shoes, they both had all their clothes on. They lay on their sides, facing each other.

"You know, the operating room was much lighter than how it looks on television."

"Yeah?"

"It wasn't dark at all. I remember being wheeled in on one of those trolley things. I don't know what they're called. And then the doctor asked me to count to twenty. I can't remember how many numbers I counted. I don't think I got up to ten. Then I woke up in this other room next to the other people, in the other beds. They'd had the operation too, I guess. I don't think it took that long but I was asleep for a while. I'm still feeling sleepy."

"Are you painful?"

"Not that much. A bit. I don't think the drugs have worn off yet. I hope it won't hurt a lot when they do. They said it was supposed to be kind of like period pain."

"I don't want you to go back to America."

"Sorry? Oh." She didn't know what to say. She wished they could talk about it another time when she was feeling clear again.

"I love you."

Why? was the first thing that came into her mind. "Thank you," she said, and squeezed his hand. Then she wondered if she should say it back but the moment had passed. She felt him move slightly away.

"I'm sorry," she said. "I'm sorry about all of this."

"It's okay," he said.

"No, it's not," she said angrily and instantly regretted her tone. Then she said something she didn't believe. "We'll meet next year after I finish school."

"Yeah?" he said, not really believing it.

"Yeah," she said with less conviction.

"You miss your friends?"

"I'm not really thinking about them at the moment."

"School is better?"

She rolled her eyes in the dark. School was the last thing on her mind. She just wanted him to hold her and he wasn't. Why couldn't he just . . . She turned over and pulled him toward her almost angrily so that he had to come closer.

But the harder they pressed together, the emptier they felt. His stomach ached where it touched her back. It was terrible to be so close and to feel far away.

Finally, he put his hand on her stomach, and she held it lower and closed her eyes. And as her hand continued to press his hand to the pain, she felt too much like a woman and he felt sick for wanting to be a boy.

35

When Amy arrived home, her family was out having Sunday yum cha. Cardboard boxes were stacked against the wall. When they got back, she told them hiking was fun, then disappeared to pack her room. She called Simon that night.

"We're leaving Wednesday."

Simon felt like he'd smashed his leg and it was just before the pain started to kick in.

"So soon," he said, too light and friendly.

"Yeah," said Amy. "Nathan can get straight back into school this way."

"Oh, that's good," he heard himself say.

"I'll miss you. Simon, thanks for going with me." Then she raised her voice all of a sudden. "I had a good time!"

"What?"

"Thank you so much."

He guessed that her mother had come into the room.

"Yeah, me too," he answered back, trying to act as well. He thought about saying good-bye then, quickly, when they weren't being themselves, but he couldn't do it.

"Okay, we have to meet somewhere before I go," she whispered.

"Yeah, of course."

She suggested the bench in Central. Tuesday afternoon.

Simon was angry on Tuesday. He didn't want to talk to anyone and he didn't want to listen to anyone. He collected his holey sweaters, books and notepapers, put them in a plastic bag, and threw the bag on his desk. Then he fished out his shoebox of English words from under his bed. The 747s were peeling off a little. He flicked through the cards once, then jammed the old shoebox in the garbage. Then he called her back.

"I want to say good-bye now."

"What?"

"I think is better."

"You don't want to meet?"

"Yeah. I don't want."

"But . . ."

"I have to work."

"Where?"

"Somewhere. You don't know."

"All right," she said in little more than a whisper. "But I made something for you."

Simon shook his head. Then he said something to hurt her.

"Give it to Jordan."

"What? Simon . . ."

"I think your mother would prefer."

Amy let out a laugh. "Maybe. But I wouldn't."

After that, she went silent and he could feel her giving up on him. He told himself to laugh quickly, but he couldn't untwist himself.

She held the phone for a while after it went silent, then started packing again, shaking her head in the nervous way her mother did.

When Simon got off the phone, he walked to his favorite place, a pedestrian bridge above the freeway, and watched the cars. But their roar no longer brought up the ocean, and their direction no longer gave him hope. They just made noise as they went by. He wanted Amy to go by too. He burst into tears for the first time in his teenage life.

Things go by, he told himself. But how he wished he'd

held on just once as tightly as he could.

His anger fell away and he thought about his last words to her, and the idea of her not knowing how he loved her. He had to speak to her one more time. He ran back to the shop.

"Amy!"

"Jordan?" came the reply.

"Hello?" he said.

"It's good to hear from you!" said Amy's mother.

"I'm . . ."

"Amy's gone out but she will be back in ten minutes. Call back then. All right?"

"Uh-huh."

"You sound so sad, Jordan. Is everything okay?"

"Yes. Fine."

36

Simon had never talked much about where he lived. Amy knew his address but didn't have a good picture of his neighborhood. He'd mostly just said it was gray.

His parents' shop was supposed to be along a back lane close to the subway station. He'd said once that they sold kitchen things, "also umbrellas," and that his father looked ancient.

"Kitchen things," she mumbled to herself as she scanned the shops. She saw a depressing clothing store with a few faded dresses in its window, then a small grocery store. A white-haired man was sitting on a crate outside.

Amy hesitated for a moment, then spoke to him in

Chinese. "Are you Simon's father?"

"Simon? Who?" he said in Chinese.

"Uh . . . Chan?" she said and realized with a pang that she didn't know his real first name. Then she saw a basket of umbrellas in front of another shop two doors down. She thanked the old man and raced over. A bell jingled as she opened the door.

"Simon?" she called softly. "Hello?"

The store smelled of old paint, tea, and Mr. Chan's lunch, the bones of which remained on a page of newspaper in front of him. He looked up at once and then returned to his reading. Amy walked down the second aisle whispering Simon's name. He'd said he lived in the back somewhere, but she couldn't see how. Then in the shadows of the first aisle she saw the beads, and a dark figure behind them.

"Simon?"

"Hm?" said the woman, drawing back the beads.

Amy acted like she'd found a bowl.

Mrs. Chan frowned. "Can I help you?"

"Is your son here?" said Amy, also in Chinese.

"Chan Tze Man?" said his mother, relaxing a little. The same face, the same eyes. "No."

His father looked over at Amy. "She is his girlfriend?"

"Be quiet, old man," Mrs. Chan said with a scowl. Then to Amy, "I don't know where he is."

"Can I leave something?" Amy continued in her shaky Chinese.

"I don't think she understands Chinese so well, this girl."

"Maybe she is not Chinese!" shouted Mr. Chan.

Mrs. Chan pointed to the small room beside her. Inside was a bunk bed and a narrow desk.

Amy sat on Simon's chair and left him a note with the words to the song she'd seen on his MP3 the first day they'd met. It was the only song he'd ever told her he liked. She'd drawn pictures along the borders. The chorus played in her head as she raced off to Central.

Can you meet me halfway, right at the borderline
That's where I'm gonna wait for you
I'll be lookin out, night and day
Took my heart to the limit, and this is where I'll stay
I can't go any further than this
I want you so bad it's my only wish

She walked up to the cobblestones and looked along restaurant row. Then she went to the bench by the water. But he wasn't there.

"You jerk!" she yelled. *Don't you understand anything? How can you not be here when I need you? You're always here when I need you.*

37

Simon was headed to the mountains. His plan was to be back by late Wednesday morning, some time after she'd gone. He figured it wouldn't be as bad if he were traveling at the same time that she was.

The bus journey was steeper and narrower than he expected. He looked out the window with some fear, ate a couple of chips.

An hour after the bus let him off at a mountain town, he wondered how much longer he needed to stay. It didn't take long to check out the shops, and he was too young to be served in a bar. He thought about looking for a cheap hostel like the one in China, but he figured if he got a room, he'd start standing up every five seconds like he'd been doing in his own room.

He caught the next bus back to Choi Hung station and from there decided to walk to the harbor. It was sure to take him several hours.

He tried to fill his mind with useless information as he walked. The questions on the English exam. The ingredients of his iced tea. He stepped over spilled food and walked through soup steam. He passed dead ducks on tree trunk cutting boards. He looked at the wooden walls of Japanese restaurants and noticed how he could never smell their food. A line of camera stores lit up the sidewalk like sunshine.

Long after dark, he made it to the street market in the area with the same name as her boyfriend. A Chinese opera was underway. Inside a three-sided hut, an actor half whined, half sang, and then someone banged a drum and rattled a rice-filled instrument. Simon didn't know what the story was about except that someone was heartbroken and angry. Simon wondered if that would be him one day, shouting a song about something that had happened a long time ago.

When he reached the water, the nightclubs and street restaurants were the only places left open. He found a bench to sit on and imagined her hands covering his eyes.

"Gotcha," she had once said.

* * *

His clothes were damp from being outside all night though the sun had been out for some time. He felt too low to be angry. She told him she was leaving in the morning. She'd be gone by now.

The shop phone rang the instant he stepped inside.

"Wei," his mother answered. Simon saw from her comprehension that the person on the other end had to be speaking Chinese. "For you."

"Ronaldo speaking," he mumbled.

"How did you know?"

"I don't have many friends who speak Chinese."

"That's because you're too weird."

"What do you mean?"

"You know what I mean."

"So what do you want?"

"Are you ready?"

"For what?"

"Simon!"

"Oh, yeah. Big exam."

"See! You're so strange. Meet you at the bus station or the hall?"

"I don't know. . . . Hall."

"Okay. Bye."

"Bye." He walked through to his room. He needed a couple of pens. His wallet. ID card. There was a note on his desk beside the large plastic bag. *Simon.*

"Oh my god."

He crashed through the beads. "Ma! What . . . ?"

"Girl."

"When?"

"Yesterday."

"Did she say anything?"

"Nothing. Poor Chinese."

"She spoke Chinese? What did she look like?"

"Small nose."

"Beautiful!" shouted his father.

Where are you? I'll be at Lai King station at 9:30 tomorrow. I have to go up to the airport express by 10:00. Please come.

"She's still here," he mumbled. "She's leaving in the late morning!" he shouted as he raced out the door and back across the bridge.

"Crazy," mumbled Mrs. Chan.

"Hah?" said Mr. Chan.

On the train Simon checked to see that he still had her iPod in his pack, and his pens.

38

The airport express was in a separate section of Lai King station. It was more high-tech looking than the local train platforms and even more spotless. Nathan remembered the TVs on the back of the airplane-like seats. He couldn't wait to get aboard. Amy looked behind her as they walked through the station. She was almost at the final escalator. Once she got on, it would be hard for him to get to her. He would have to buy a ticket to the airport to get through. Her mother and brother stepped on.

"Amy!" called her mother.

She let the escalator take her away. She couldn't believe it. *Where are you?* She kept looking down but he didn't come.

At the top, they scanned through and the metal turnstile snapped shut behind them.

"Yay!" said Nathan as the train warning rang followed by the airport express. "Can we sit in front?"

"Just wait till we get on," said Mrs. Lee.

Everyone began to move forward.

"These trains leave every twenty minutes, right?" Amy asked a Chinese woman in English. The woman acted like she didn't hear.

First the platform doors opened and then the train doors opened. Amy took another look at the turnstiles. She caught her breath as someone came up to buy a ticket. But it wasn't him. Another passenger bumped her from behind. She climbed on after her mom and Nathan, just inside the doors. An old couple was having trouble getting their luggage inside. Then the aisle cleared and everyone started to walk through.

"Mom!" Amy called out. "Don't worry. I'll be there."

"What? Where are you going?"

Nathan felt her squeeze his shoulder, then she was gone and the doors were shut.

"Please step back from the doors," the recording blared.

He stopped asking people the time. He wasn't going to give up. "She needs her music," he mumbled to himself for the hundredth time. It had to be at least five minutes past ten, he figured. The train doors took long seconds to let him out at Lai King. Then he was all eyes. Nothing but signs filled his mind. Airport Express? He found the right escalator. At the bottom he heard a departure recording playing at the top.

He flew up the escalator steps. But when he made it to the gate, the train doors had closed.

"No!" he yelled.

He searched for her face as the train started to move. Then he saw her running toward him along the platform.

"Simon!" she screamed.

"Amy!"

He lifted himself over the turnstile and took off. She cried out again when she saw him running toward her. Then they were in each other's arms.

"You're here," she whispered.

"Yes."

Then she punched him. "What TOOK you?"

"I don't know."

"What were you DOING?"

"I don't know. Walking."

"Walking? Where?"

"Many place . . . places."

"You weren't going to see me?"

He shook his head.

"But I need you!"

"Don't go," he said. "Don't leave. I can't . . ." But he couldn't speak.

"Simon . . ."

"Yeah, I know. I just wanted to see you. That's all."

"Me too." she said, still holding on to him. "Shit. What about your exam? Did Katie call you?"

"Yes."

"So you're going?"

"Yes, I'm going. . . . What about you? Will you miss your plane now?"

"I don't know. I think I can catch another train."

"I'll come with you."

"Will you have time?"

"Yes, there is a lot of time before my exam."

"Are you sure?"

"Yes. Sure."

She scowled at him and he scowled back.

On the train, they held each other tight.

39

The airport terminal was a great hall made of glass and steel. They stayed close. Simon carried her bag. Mrs. Lee was waiting at the airline counter. She did her nervous nod, then said something under her breath as she spotted her daughter. Nathan ran over when he saw her.

"I told you not to worry," Amy said as she hugged him.

"But you could have missed the plane! Mom was going to kill you."

She patted his head. "No, it's okay."

They walked to the line for checking in baggage. Mrs. Lee had fixed it so her daughter could go to the front.

"This way!" she said. "Hurry up."

Simon looked around but not at Mrs. Lee. He winked at Nathan. Amy took his hand when she finished checking in. He looked at her seat number.

"Ah, window," he said.

Her hand felt different now. He didn't want to press as hard as before, but then she did and he did back.

They talked as they walked through the terminal. He would have no memory of what they said. He noticed there was no line in front of the international gates.

She told her mother to go ahead.

Her mother broke into a torrent of Chinese. "Enough. Your mother is tired now. It is time to obey."

"Mom, I'll come in a minute. I'm not gonna miss the plane. I promise. Okay?"

"Come on," said Mrs. Lee. Then she took her son's hand and walked through.

Simon looked pale. "You understand Chinese?"

"A little," she said sheepishly, and buried herself in his arms again. "It was better for your English."

He started to laugh. "I can't believe."

"We'll use it as our secret code when you come to America."

"Okay."

And the complete trust in his eyes made her cry.

"Don't worry," he told her.

"But it shouldn't be like this. I don't want to leave you here."

"I don't want you to leave. . . . Your music!" he said, then swung around his backpack. "Here. Take." And he put her iPod in her bag.

"No!" she said, some fire returning to her eyes.

"Yes. You need."

"No. You have to play my music."

"Every music is remind me of you." Then he frowned. "I didn't give you anything."

"What do you mean? Are you crazy? . . . Simon!"

He shook his head. He wasn't convinced.

"I love you," she said.

He felt like Superman and he felt like crying.

"I love you," he told her. This time, he knew she really heard him.

They held each other and their faces mixed warm and salty. He kissed her on her eyes and on her cheeks and then they kissed slowly and they knew it was the last one and she breathed him in. Then they let go.

He saw her once through the closing doors. There were people everywhere, most standing in line with their passports out. She was on the other side now in her mother's arms with her brother hugging her legs.

He smiled but he hurt all over. He wandered back to the

trains. He shook a little. His heart was pounding. A wave of people emerged from behind a wall of sliding doors. He saw the train platform behind them and looked back once more at the airport. He thought about how close she was, even though she was gone. He pictured her boarding her plane, sitting down in her window seat, looking for him. Then he realized there was one last thing he had to do before he left. He looked for the doors to the outside.

Her plane was supposed to be mostly white, with a little red. It was one of the airlines he'd had on his shoebox. Damn it, he thought, and hoped no one had thrown in any food since he'd put his box in the garbage.

He ran along the outside of the terminal until he reached a clearing at the far side of the car park.

Her plane was paused at the top of a distant runway like it was waiting for him to notice. Then it charged toward the sky.

"Go smooth! Fly strong!"

He followed her until his sight clouded over and he could barely see at all. But as her plane disappeared, he felt it in his bones that life was moving, and big and beyond what anyone could see. Then out of the blue, her plane reappeared. And as Amy soared above him, Simon jumped high and waved his arms. Out tumbled his old MP3 player, come back to life once more.

Acknowledgments

My grateful thanks are due to Emily Hazel for finding SG, and to George Nicholson for finding the best of homes. To HarperCollins's Phoebe Yeh, super editor, for showing me how to make a book light without losing the weight of the story, and her super team, Jayne Carapezzi and Amanda Glickman. To JY muse, my parents, my brother Michael, Brooks McLaren, Phaidra Speirs, Debbie Levy, Aybays, and RARR, thank you for your brains, love, and encouragement. And thanks to the dream cast of *A Wing, Wu?*, Carmen, Paola, and Paschali; Form 4C of SKH Tsoi Kung Po 2000/1; and the real Katie and Kenny.